Moondrop to Murder

by the same author

Superintendent Kenworthy novels

PASSION IN THE PEAK
THE HOBBEMA PROSPECT
CORRIDORS OF GUILT
THE ASKING PRICE
THE SUNSET LAW
THE GREEN FRONTIER
SURRENDER VALUE
PLAYGROUND OF DEATH
THE ANATHEMA STONE
SOME RUN CROOKED
NO BIRDS SANG
HANGMAN'S TIDE
DEATH IN MIDWINTER
DEATH OF AN ALDERMAN

Inspector Brunt novels

THE QUIET STRANGER
MR FRED
DEAD-NETTLE
GAMEKEEPER'S GALLOWS
RESCUE FROM THE ROSE

JOHN BUXTON HILTON

Moondrop to Murder

A Superintendent Kenworthy novel

St. Martin's Press
New York

Library of Congress Cataloging in Publication Data

Hilton, John Buxton.
  Moondrop to murder.

  I. Title.
PR6058.I5M55 1986   823'.914   86-1823
ISBN 0-312-54699-8

First published in Great Britain by William Collins Sons & Co. Ltd.
First U.S. Edition
10 9 8 7 6 5 4 3 2 1

Moondrop to Murder

CHAPTER 1

If it was going to be an old case over again, Kenworthy did not want it. It was interfering too rawly in a man's business, minding him at his wife's expense while his last fling probably came to nothing.

His first sight of the Neville residence did not make up his mind for him. Agnes Neville was in her well-managed sixties, tending to overweight but not desperately so, neat, self-confident—and in no material want. She was well aware of this but without complacency. She was not a woman ever likely to accept less than she asked for; nor to be backward about asking. She said nothing direct about her relationship with Neville, leaving Kenworthy to find his way from one surmise to another.

The home was on the Warwickshire-Gloucestershire borders, a split-level bungalow that commanded a rolling dip in the Cotswolds. The room in which Agnes Neville received Kenworthy had space enough for a concert grand to be in nobody's way. There was Poulenc open on the music-rack —a *Bagatelle* that to Kenworthy's eye looked extraordinarily difficult—both to play and to listen to. An escritoire must surely be eighteenth-century French and beyond price. Except for photographs, everything on the wall was either an original or a numbered print: he had heard of none of the artists. There were a few abstracts, some he could have lived with. He was a man who liked to see a touch of reason behind splodges of satisfying colour.

Such affluence from a chain of dry-cleaning businesses in provincial market towns? For that was as romantic as Colonel Rawdon Neville's post-war break-out had been. (Though he had been a regular soldier, he did not use the title of his rank in civilian life and there was no memento of his service anywhere about his home.) Kenworthy had looked into the Army List, since Neville did not rise to *Who's Who* or even a compendium of county notables. He had graduated from Sandhurst in 1930, with a brevet majority a few months before the outbreak of war, had passed Staff College after Dunkirk. The entry, after Kenworthy had decoded the abbreviations, had done little to reveal the man. He had drawn his bowler hat in 1946 from the same slightly lower-drawer regiment in which he had been gazetted: a Fish 'n' Chip Mob, in the eyes of the élite.

Neville, now in his seventies, must be something like ten years older than his wife. From the evidence of photographs about the room, this had been a second marriage for both of them. Among the framed groups there was a bride who had just been given away by a man who bore no resemblance to Neville: she had the same chubby prettiness that her mother might once have had: the same hint of inelasticity about what she required from life. She would be cold, hard and confident about her targets.

Kenworthy was sitting at the wrong angle to pry for pictorial evidence of the first Mrs Neville: as far as he could see, there was none. In some company he would simply have got up and inspected the family gallery head-on, but Agnes Neville's disposition did not encourage this. It was not that he was afraid of offending her. He did indeed find something initially stifling in her self-assurance—but if he did not want to interest himself, he did not have to. For the time being he was content to allow her presence to command the tone of the interview. It seemed a reasonably informative way of letting things develop.

She had finished telling him what it was about: that Rawdon had been to his doctor three weeks ago. After a couple of days of tests (in a private clinic, it went without saying) he had come back with the obvious knowledge that he had something perfectly ghastly wrong with him. He had not told her what it was. If he didn't want to tell her, she wouldn't expect him to: that was indicative of their relationship. It seemed she wouldn't have thought of putting pressure on him. Kenworthy also thought it worth noting that they did not go to the same doctor. They did not live in the kind of interdependence that was married life as he understood it.

'So he has an appointment with his surgeon on the tenth of the month after next. He's given me no details—perhaps it's best not to know too much. But it's obvious that it is— what ought I to call it—ante-penultimate?'

An odd choice of word: it was the first time she had departed from plain, unsentimental essentials; and she still said it plainly and without sentiment.

'So he's off on a month's walking tour in the south of France—a route he followed during a vacation in his officer-cadet days. He says it will take his mind off the operation—and deliver him to the theatre in the pink of physical condition.'

'Will his health stand up to a walking tour?'

Or was it a St John Ambulance man that she should be setting on his shadow?

'There's nothing wrong with his heart and lungs.'

Neville's yardstick of outward fitness was apparent from a portrait in oils done in his early twenties by a competent amateur. It showed a boundingly big man, so aggressively on top of his health that he must have made many a passer-by feel something of a weed. And that must have been as true in the regimental mess as it was in the street.

'And what precisely do you want me to do?'

'Be not too far away. Just in case.'

'I suppose it would be possible to tail a fellow Englishman for a month about the South of France. It wouldn't be easy, operating singly. And presumably it wouldn't do for him to know?'

'He's unaware that I'm in touch with you, and if he does catch you on his heels, he'll undoubtedly explode. If that happens, explode back at him and wait for him to simmer down. Actually, I think you and he might get on reasonably well.'

Was there, despite contrary indications, a touch of humour in her make-up? She must know that what she was asking was well-nigh impossible.

'So if he blows my cover, your real hope is that we'll journey together like old friends? But I'm not to let him know who's commissioned me?'

She summoned up a smile. It suggested struggling patience rather than sympathy.

'I don't know who else he'd think it might be. That would be up to you, according to circumstances. We are all three of us *adult*, Mr Kenworthy.'

Kenworthy looked out of the window at a lawn mown and pegged for croquet.

'And that's all there is to it?' he asked her directly.

'Isn't that enough? If you fancy he will not keep you on your toes, knowing my husband—'

'That isn't what I meant. Is the state of his health the only thing that worries you?'

Again she said it: 'Isn't that enough?'

She wouldn't be a safe woman to trifle with. She would know she was being trifled with before one started.

'I don't know,' she said. 'I have no way of knowing how sick he is. I want someone ubobtrusively in the offing.'

'Then for one thing, you had better make quietly sure that he has the right kind of travel insurance. It might cost a lot of money to bring him home in an air-ambulance.'

'He'll have looked after all that kind of thing for himself, Mr Kenworthy. He is—what's the word?—assiduous.' *picky*

Did that imply that she had suffered one woman's share of Neville's assiduity?

'You are my way of being quietly sure of any odd thing he might not have thought of.'

She was retaining something—so he had to oppose her.

'Mrs Neville, if I thought you were holding anything back—'

'What sort of thing do you think I might be holding back?'

She was beginning to be irritated. She might be suffering some element of suppressed shock at the news about her husband's state of health. But she must have known for years that this moment was likely to come.

'Mr Kenworthy, let us be honest. He probably believes that he is under sentence of death. Who was it said that that composes a man? He is going walking in France to come to terms with one thing or another. Perhaps he will have a thick night or two—'

'Is he a drinking man?

'Socially. Modestly. But he enjoyed himself when he was young. And he is going back to where he was young. He might try to repeat history.'

'Has he strong associations with France?'

'He has always talked of our going there next year. He'd get maps and guide-books out—but when it came to contacting the travel agent, he unobtrusively put it off. It's been like that ever since we married—that's twelve years. And I know you are reluctant to ask—we both have previous experience. We believe we are both above the more obvious mistakes.'

'And earlier in his life? He often crossed the Channel?'

'I have never cross-examined him about it.'

'Yet you gave the impression just now that he is a Franco-phile.'

'You could say he is. With reservations. He was in France during the war.'

'In the South? Special Operations, perhaps? *Kenworthy wondered*.

'He speaks French?' *she asked.*

'Excellently.'

There was a pause. She was ready for the interview to come to a finish. But then she had second thoughts.

'Mr Kenworthy, you're fishing for something. There *is*

something. I don't know what it is, either. That's why I
want you to stay near him.'

Kenworthy's mind kept coming back in circles to the
relationship between this couple. Until this affliction,
Neville had kept himself an outstandingly fit man. So he'd
be a man with healthy—and continuing—appetites. There
was nothing ebulliently sexy about his wife. But she was a
woman who would know the *quid pro quo's*. She looked
Kenworthy in the eye, knowing the way his mind was
working.

'Of course, it has crossed my mind that there might be a
woman that he's curious to see again. I'm not sending you
to find that out. What you tell me when you come back is
a matter for your discretion. I know the code of honour
between men. You needn't tell me anything, if that's how
you feel about it. Your job is to do what you can to see that
he does come back. If there is something that he feels he
has to round off, I don't begrudge it him. He is a man of
codes and protocols. He would have enjoyed himself at
Arthur's table.'

And now she relaxed into a fleetingly broad smile, though
she made sure that it was fleeting.

'After all, she'll be in her seventies too, won't she?'

Two fledgling starlings quarrelled over a morsel on the
lawn.

'So you are prepared to do this for me, Mr Kenworthy?
I'm afraid I can't give you long to think it over—count it
in hours. If it doesn't appeal to you, I shall have to find
someone to whom it does, and that might not be easy.'

She was a woman with whom one did business on her
terms. Time to think it over would mean time to consider
how difficult it might be—how embarrassing and how likely
to end up in an untidy showdown. The six feet four of
stamina and sinew in that oil-painting looked as if Neville
might indeed explode, if he found he was being spied on.
This was probably going to be his last spell of privacy.

'You were saying just now that there *is* something,' Kenworthy said.

'You were quizzing me about how fond he is of France. I'd say very fond indeed. And reluctant ever to talk about it. Or, if it came to the crunch, go there again.'

'And this was something arising from his war service?'

'I have always had the feeling that something uncomfortable happened—something that he has never been happy about. And I do assure you—he is the most unresentful of men.'

'I'll do it,' Kenworthy said. 'Provided there are no surprise clauses in my brief.'

'I have given you your brief, Mr Kenworthy.'

He had suspected that once he accepted, she might release what she was withholding. But she added nothing. She went to the escritoire and brought out a folded sheet of notepaper.

'Here are the details of his flight. To Nice. I have had to pry in his papers to find that. After Nice, he seems to mean to play it as it comes. If he has any fixed plans, he's kept them to himself. I don't even know whether he has booked himself into a hotel. You haven't asked about expenses. You needn't. Claim from me what you need, when you need it. I take it you'll use Eurocheques? Just let me know the details of your account. I'll keep it primed.'

CHAPTER 2

Kenworthy's French was rusty but not quite seized up. He flew to Nice to acclimatize himself, two days before Neville was due. He had hardly looked at a word of the language since Normandy, and that was—God help him!—not far short of forty years ago. He struggled through a couple of Simenons while Elspeth was failing to get a sensible answer about what she ought to pack for him. It was March, and

a damp, peevish cold pervaded England. He tried to pull
her leg about the Riviera sunshine. She said it would be
chilly in the mountains, especially at night. But a gratifying
warmth embraced him as he came out across the forecourt
of Nice's maritime airport: broad beds of cyclamen in boldly
contrasting colours.

He took to Nice. He liked the openness, the activity, the
style. He had expected to run into big-spenders on every
corner, but the Carnival was over and there was a lull before
the beach and marina season. He found instead an evoca-
tive nineteeth-century backcloth, well-dressed geriatric
promenaders—and nostalgic hints of the Victorian heights
of English tourism. He booked in at a small hotel off the
Avenue Jean Médecin, went to a cinema and sat through
the same film three times. It was a police procedural and
by the third repetition he was anticipating whole chunks of
dialogue.

He drank gaseous beer at zinc counters, under no illusions
about the initial pick-up. It was going to be tricky: not a
job for one man, he had told Agnes Neville. Someone at the
Yard had recommended the Agence St Hubert: well, Hubert
was the patron saint of hunters, an auspicious start. He had
written for an appointment before leaving London and found
the private eye's bureau on a dusty back landing surrounded
by second-hand furniture shops in a *quartier* east of the main
railway station. The ambience was in no way reminiscent
of the Côte d'Azur, and the office was deserted except for a
typist who could find no note anywhere that he was expected. She was candidly and disconcertingly sexy, would
have looked more in place on a beach mattress than at a
desk. Her skirt set off a pair of legs that in some walks of
life would have been worth insuring.

'I have an appointment with Monsieur Raoul Verdier.'

She went and looked on the boss's desk, came back
uninformed. Her blouse accentuated a bosom of which she
seemed unconscious, and her complexion had a permanent

tan from round-the-calendar sunshine. Her perfume was vertiginous. Kenworthy was not given to lusting after passing vessels, but if he had been the type, at a more active age this one could have filled his bill: he tried not to let her catch him looking directly at her. She knew the effect she had on men, and not far under the surface, she was highly amused by it. She listened to him with that false admiration with which the French polite classes like to reward courageous efforts in their language. She herself moved over into fluent English.

'Where did you learn to speak French without accent, monsieur?'

Bullshit. He wanted no waste of time in small-talk. She said that she did not expect Monsieur Verdier in again today and that all the partners were out on assignments. But of course she would take a message, and he could rely on someone from the Agence to carry out his wishes. It was really only a matter, Kenworthy told her, of covering an hour or two tomorrow, shadowing a man from the airport and keeping tabs on him while he himself moved his gear from his present hotel to somewhere where he could keep a closer eye on him.

The girl nodded, as if to suggest that she was already several stages ahead of him and did not really need to listen. She had started making notes, but added a very few after the first few words. He did not think she was wearing a bra.

Evidemment: she was sure that Monsieur Verdier or one of the senior partners would attend to this himself. If the assignment had been accepted, then it would be carried out. *Aucun problème*. Kenworthy emerged into uninvigorating sunshine, unhappy in his lack of faith. It had been a stimulating experience, talking to this young lady, but in the wrong way. She did not inspire professional confidence, and if the Agence let him down, then Neville was likely to give him the slip before he had crossed the city.

The next morning he walked kilometres to the *Aéroport*,

along the showpiece Promenade des Anglais. From Cap
Ferrat to St Laurent the long line of kid-gloved waves was
breaking on sands not yet organized for the affluent season.
Beyond the sea lay Africa: he found that difficult to believe.
North of the city loomed the *massif* of the Alpes Maritimes,
peppered with the villas of the millionaire fringe. It was
surely in the wild mountain country beyond that he was
going to have to walk a marathon on Neville's heels. Was
it to be a fight against personal embarrassments—or a damp
squib? Would it prove no more than one man's sentimental
pilgrimage—and an old man at that, his last snap at nostal-
gia? Or was Agnes Neville right: there was more to it than
that?

Standing behind a pillar at the Aéroport, Kenworthy
watched the oldest trick in the pickpockets' repertoire—a
man jostled by two others, his wallet changing ownership.
Dead easy, if he would keep it in the back pocket of his
jeans. It was none of Kenworthy's business—which was
almost a luxury in itself. Then he caught his first sight of
his man as he came out through the Customs. They were
stopping about one in twenty and did not bother Neville.

He was almost a caricature of the bowler-hatted British
colonel: clean-shaven, but for a moustache clipped almost
down to bristle, steel-grey eyebrows and a forward gait that
reminded one of a tank disregarding road-blocks. Kenworthy remembered a 1939 photograph of the two First
World War heroes who were going to shoulder the first
appalling failure of the Second: Ironside and Gort, in immaculate jodhpurs and riding boots, confident to the point
of arrogance. Gort had the VC, a regular soldier's regular
soldier. Neither of them had appeared to believe in the
reality of Blitzkrieg.

Neville gave the same impression. Self-satisfied, undoubtedly a man with a code, a man of honour, of decency.
Perhaps of an evening, over modest cups, you could talk
new ideas to Neville and he would give every impression of

seeing your point. But the morning after, over a stonily silent breakfast, he would be back with the book of precedents, playing all things safe—heading for failure with all his excuses ready. Kenworthy had never conceived any great love for colonels.

Neville came out into the main concourse, looked about himself with essentially English eyes, seeing it all, but ignoring what he did not think affected him, barged through the wrong door and went to the wrong desk for what he wanted: asking at the Hertz bureau for a taxi. A woman of the type that Kenworthy knew as well as he knew Neville's came out of the Douane and headed for the exit. She was one of those characters that one can see travelling any day of the week, undaunted by jet aircraft in her late seventies, on her way to make life uncomfortable for a daughter-in-law. And despite the fact that she was walking with her feet turned painfully inwards, leaning forward with a stoop on a rubber-ferruled stick, she was making a fair pace: until the Filipino wickerwork basket that she was carrying fell open.

A bottle of Lucien Lelong was shattered star-wise on the parquet. A packet of king-size filter-tips went one way, a Colibri lighter another; and paper tissues, lipsticks, compact and keys, nail varnish and a mirror, together with a plastic concertina of credit cards and a British passport were scattered under the feet of men pushing baggage trolleys. Kenworthy plunged downward and retrieved first the passport, then the credit cards. Someone's toe stubbed a miniature Hennessy and sent it skidding. Others had come to the old dear's help and a woman in airport uniform was helping her across to a seat with an armful of her belongings.

The outcome was that by the time Kenworthy had reached the gratifying mildness of the outside air, he saw Colonel Neville in a taxi in mid-stream, being driven to a destination that could be miles away. A looming minibus changed lanes at exactly the right moment to obscure the taxi's number-plates. A few years ago, Kenworthy would have had the balls off any detective-constable who lost a man in such conditions.

There is only one way an officer could achieve that, my friend— by rank incompetence—

He lost sight of the taxi beyond the flowerbed pincushion of a roundabout. It was at least four miles to the city centre, and he would be at least three places back in the taxi queue. Assessing it at the lowest grade of failure, it was going to be a costly business in terms of fees and expenses that he had no moral right to claim.

The old woman with her wicker basket could well be in Neville's employ. If she was, she could not have chosen a more critical spot or moment for her bag to come undone. And that introduced two new thoughts: that Neville knew that Kenworthy was going to be marking him; and that he wanted rid of Kenworthy.

Kenworthy looked at the jostling pavements of central Nice and knew that it was hopeless. He went back to his hotel room in ineffective fury. There was no way of knowing whether Neville would stay in Nice overnight or travel immediately to his next jumping-off spot. If Kenworthy went drifting round the more obvious places that an Englishman might want to visit after a long exile from the Riviera, there might just be some coincidental chance that he might come across him—

Then the phone rang on Kenworthy's bedroom wall. Who the hell would be ringing him here? Who *knew* that he was here? Kenworthy did not like French telephones. French consonants tended to get lost in French ear-pieces. He did not even recognize the woman's voice.

'Monique Colin.'

'I think—'

'*De l'Agence St Hubert*,' she said.

'Ah—Hubert the hunter who stayed home.'

'No. Our *Agence* never stays at home. I was at the *Aéroport* just now. I saw you run to help the old lady.'

Kenworthy crossed his fingers.

'This line is bad,' she said. 'Can you meet me in ten minutes' time? I'm in the—'

Some bar whose name he could not catch.

'*Où ça?*'

'Not a hundred metres from your hotel. Corner of the Rue du Taupe and the Rue des Requins.'

It was a small place, without other customers. The girl from the agency was wearing a waist-length synthetic fur and had pulled wrinkled leg-warmers over her tights. Her perfume seemed even headier than before and Kenworthy felt uneasy, sitting close to her. She looked at him and laughed.

'I'm afraid the old lady distracted your attention.'

'There are times when *noblesse* has no business to *oblige*. Let's hope she didn't distract yours. Was it contrived, do you think?'

'For sure.'

'But did you see where Colonel Neville went?'

She produced a small notebook and tore out a page.

'I hope you do not object to the smell of fish.'

'That depends on any number of factors. Proximity, age, degree of confinement. Why—has the Colonel found himself a billet in a canning factory?'

'No—but he asked the taxi-driver for the Hôtel des Deux Chèvres—that's among the fish-markets. There's another small hotel almost opposite: the Pot au Feu. From there you should be able to pick him up again easily enough. I've booked a room there for you. They'll let it go again, if you're not there by seven. It's not far from the bus station, so they don't often have vacancies. You were lucky.'

'Very,' he said. 'And I'm not referring to the hotel.'

She really was the most luscious little dish that he'd sat in a bar with for years. He wondered just how smugly she was laughing up her sleeve at his ineptitude.

'Colonel Neville,' he asked her, 'would be quite unaware of your interest in him?'

'He seemed quite relaxed—once you were on your hands and knees among the scent-bottles. And by the way, Monsieur Verdier asked me to tell you that if you need further help, we do consider ourselves mobile.'

She handed him a professional card. He was conscious of her laughing eyes—and of her impossibly competent youthfulness.

CHAPTER 3

The two hotels, at right angles to each other, overlooked the cobbled Place du Toison d'Or in the narrow tangle of the Old Town. The Place could not have been more than a hundred metres square and in its centre stood three plane trees and the bust of some nineteeth-century luminary from whose pedestal water ran from iron pipes into three over-brimming basins. A pigeon was defiling the dignitary's head while surveying a potential mate with a lecherous orange eye. Earlier in the day there had been a market in the square. Its stalls were now stripped and everything in sight had been copiously washed down. All places of business appeared to be closed—shops and cafés emptily dead behind shutters that had not been painted for donkeys' years. It seemed impossible that life would ever return to the Place.

Kenworthy's Hôtel du Pot au Feu, undistinguished by a single star, was basic but clean, and in its own-worldly way not unfriendly. Neville's Deux Chèvres looked even more humble. It was narrower and rose to fewer storeys under a Roman-tiled roof commanded by chimneys, cowls and television aerials of every style and dignity.

Kenworthy sat at the window and began a letter to

Elspeth, the hours marked by a distant and not too sound-hearted church clock. Neville put in no appearance, either at any of the windows of the Deux Chèvres or through its front door. At seven o'clock six youths arrived on mopeds, from which they had removed the silencers, and went into committee round the fountain. At ten minutes to eight a door opened under a Restaurant sign on the third side of the Place and a little man with round shoulders dragged a Menu board out on to the pavement. There was a table in the window at street-level from which Kenworthy need not lose sight of the deux Chèvres, and by ten past eight he was sitting there. Five minutes later, Neville came in and sat down at the same table.

'Mind if I join you? I might as well take a look at what I'm supposed to be lumbered with. Come to that, it's only fair for you to do the same. I take it you have an accomplice, otherwise you'd have thrown in the towel by now.'

Kenworthy nodded politely.

'I thought I'd managed to lose you at the airport,' Neville said.

His tone was courteously factual, accompanied by no smile.

'I congratulate you on your chivalrous treatment of the good lady, Kenworthy. I must say, I feared you'd be a harder man than that, when you had a job to do.'

'I used to be,' Kenworthy said. 'I'm growing soft in my old age.'

'Old? You're not old.'

And Neville recited the date of Kenworthy's birth, of his military service, and of his promotions in the Met.

'I see you've done your homework, Colonel Neville.'

'Would you have expected me not to? It must have been one of your guiding principles in your heyday: know your enemy.'

'I'm not your enemy, Colonel—unless you insist.'

'That's very civil of you.'

'Don't hold it against me for being here, Neville. No man's motives could be more altruistic.'

'I suppose it's possible to look on it that way. No doubt my dear wife felt she had to employ someone, and I don't fault her judgement in settling on you. But she might have been a little more efficient, if she really didn't want me to know what she was up to: screwed up drafts of letters in her waste-paper basket, scribbles on the telephone-pad. Since I found out, some of the information I've dug out about you might bring blushes to your cheek.'

'I'm hoping we can come to a gentlemen's agreement, Colonel.'

'Not yet awhile, we won't. We won't make up our minds about anything tonight. You're a menace to my privacy, Kenworthy. It's up to you to show me why I should prefer your company to solitude. If you can't do that, you remain hostile.'

Was it possible to picture Neville as a domestic bully? Surely that would not get him far with the woman who had interviewed Kenworthy? Or was her façade a brittle defence, deployed permanently in advance?'

'Let us not question anyone's good faith,' Neville said. 'But may Heaven protect us from Girl Guides.'

The *patron* came for their orders. It was one of those family houses where Madame handled the money, brother-in-law cooked and *Grand'mère* did the washing up. The menu was limited and the cuisine splendid. Kenworthy had *hors d'oeuvres variés*, ox tongue in Marsala sauce, a slice of Cantal and a carafe of house wine.

'So—we've checked up on each other. And I don't suppose that either of us has penetrated to the things that matter. We might start from the fact that I was a Lieutenant-Colonel and you were a Sergeant. Or if you find that invidious: you were a Chief Superintendent while I was letting a small string of dry-cleaning shops run themselves.'

He had ordered *Tripes Niçoises*, an unæsthetic-looking

dish, to which he applied himself with gusto. Evidently his medical trouble was not digestive.

'Why dry-cleaning? It wasn't a family business. I haven't even that excuse. I had a little to invest in 1946, decided I couldn't face anything more adventurous.'

'After what kinds of adventure?' Kenworthy asked him. 'The Army List misses out all the exciting bits.'

'Exciting? The only Field Service Pocket Book soldiering I did was as temporary, acting, emergency brigade major in the *drôle de guerre* before Dunkirk. Which meant trying to interpret the brigadier's thought for the day to regimental commanders significantly my seniors.'

'You were back in France later on, though.'

'In 1944. Corps staff. Trying to estimate casualties in advance. Somebody had to. Could have been a useful job —if anyone had taken notice of my figures. I soon learned that if I produced an answer that suggested calling off an attack, I was sent back to my penthouse to do the sum a different way.'

'Northern France in '39. Normandy in '44,' Kenworthy said. 'And in between?'

Neville mopped up juices with a corner of breadcrust.

'I don't know yet whether I'm going to tell you anything about what happened in between. Maybe I shan't—even if I do invite you to come for a long walk with me. How fit are you?'

'I'm sixty-two. I feel sixty-two—neither more nor less.'

'Can you still walk twenty miles in a day?'

'I dare say I'd blister a bit at first.'

'How do you believe in treating blisters?'

'Tread them in,' Kenworthy said, a treatment recommended by the MO of an Infantry Training Depot getting on for half a century ago. The answer seemed to please Neville.

'Do you love England?' he asked suddenly.

It sounded like something out of a Buchan novel. How

was Kenworthy expected to react? It struck him that Neville took himself absurdly seriously. Or was it perhaps not quite so absurd as that?

'I think so,' he said carefully. 'I get bloody exasperated sometimes.'

'About what sort of things?'

'I used to blame most of our troubles on Rock and Roll —then on the Beatles and the Stones. I know of course that that's confusing the symptoms with the disease.'

'So what's the disease? The Coloureds trying to take us over? The Arabs? The Unions?'

It was an odd political discussion: a cut and thrust of words for the sake of provoking and exploring. Both men had trodden walks of life that were notorious for producing reactionaries. Neither man was a reactionary—at least, Kenworthy did not think that Neville was at heart—but they both knew the catch-phrases. They argued from false analogies and in outrageous paradoxes, each changing his stance at intervals so as to continue to oppose the other. It was the most absurd political discussion that one could imagine between two intelligent men: yet any observer would have taken them for deadly serious. They had coffee. Neville introduced Kenworthy to a *vieux marc de Bourgogne*.

'It should suit you. It was Maigret's favourite tipple. Kenworthy—I believe that conversationally you could be quite a joy to me. I've half a mind to try you out. We could trigger off all sorts of nonsense in each other. Let's have an easy day tomorrow. We both need to play ourselves in. We'll take a bus for the first lap—until we've shaken off the conurbations.'

Kenworthy was awake a very few minutes after five. The racket under his window, around the fountain, tested credibility: a clapped-out lorry, the hammering of trestles, transistor radios—and above everything else the stridency of peasant voices exchanging comic insults. He watched for a fascinated hour the evolution of the market: Mediterranean fish of every shape and hue—barrel-shaped, sword-beaked, grotesque, elongated and chubby: crustaceans, clams, sea-urchins and nameless shellfish by the mountain-load. And the men and women of the stalls looked like immigrants from Breughel country, with the odd pirate and escapee from Devil's Island here and there among them.

Across the Place he saw Neville, also at his window. The Colonel caught sight of him, and raised an arm in acknowledgement. Kenworthy withdrew into his bedroom, washed, shaved and made short work of packing his light bag. Shortly after seven he rang for coffee and croissants to be brought to his room. And at seven-twenty he saw Neville come out of the door of the Deux Chèvres, in shorts and an open-necked shirt, with a pack on his back and swinging a walking-stick with a swagger. He walked up the lane that led back to the modern city. So he had decided on a flying start—and to jettison Kenworthy?

Kenworthy had not ceased to be a trier, but he was a realist. If Neville wanted to off-load him, everything was in the Colonel's favour. He had spoken of taking a bus today, and clearly he was on his way towards that bus now. A bus to where? To what *village perché*, somewhere in the mountains? Kenworthy had done what he could. Kenworthy would make token inquiries at the bus station, see about a flight to Heathrow the day after tomorrow—and find more things like fish markets to look at in the intervening hours.

It was easy to sit back and think of a dozen reasons for being relieved to be free of Neville. The man had a conceit that Kenworthy could not take. It was not the stage-managed arrogance of the Teuton jackboot or the Brigade of Guards. It was not the arrogance of class. It was the arrogance of a man who has thought himself into all his final positions and was too wearied by the counter-arguments to be prepared to listen to them again. It was impossible to be Neville's keeper without Neville's agreement. It would take a squad, not a lone wanderer, to keep track of an unwilling Neville. Kenworthy was in the act of paying his bill when Neville came up behind him, still wearing his rucksack.

'Hullo. You off? Had second thoughts? Chickening out?'

'I saw you leave the Deux Chèvres, and assumed you'd decided to go it alone. If that's how you want it, Neville, I'll say Amen. The dice has to come up your side.'

'Kenworthy—what sort of a shit do you think I am? If I say we'll go for a walk together, do I look the sort to chuck a dummy?'

Explode back, Mrs Neville had said.

'My trouble is, Neville, that I haven't had time yet to decide precisely what kind of shit you are.'

'Oh, scrub round it,' Neville said. 'Sorry, old man. We don't know each other. How can we? We shall do, before we're through—perhaps. I just took a stroll round the block to test the balance of this thing—get all the straps and buckles *comme il faut*.'

He swung his rucksack to the floor and made some slight adjustments. It was small, light, and made of gay blue canvas on a tubular frame.

'You don't *carry* a rucksack, Kenworthy—it has to be an extension of your body. What sort of gear have you got?'

Kenworthy had what he had travelled from Heathrow in, plus a minimal change of underwear.

'Mind if I take a look at your shoes?'

Kenworthy found himself raising his feet from the ground one after the other, while Neville inspected them. He felt as if he were a horse being examined by a blacksmith. Neville grunted at intervals, as if he had never encountered such inept footwear in his life.

'How far do you think you're going to walk in these? Twice along the sea-front at Littlehampton? And I don't suppose you thought of bringing a sleeping-bag? I know I've got a bloody cheek, Kenworthy. But this is *my* trip. If you're to come, it's on my terms—and that includes your equipment.'

'I'll not argue with that.'

'I like to make a proper job of things I do. And I suppose you'll not want to be dossing in distant inns while I'm taking a nature cure in the woods and fields. You'd be scared I wouldn't be there when you came to pick me up the next morning.'

Kenworthy did not know whether Neville was taking the Mickey out of him or not.

'You'll need a light bivouac, a bigger supply of spare socks than I expect you've brought. Cooking utensils we can share. What would you be like on a desert island, Kenworthy?'

'One of my records would be a vintage Crosby. And I'd have Kathleen Ferrier singing *Blow the wind southerly*.'

'Tino Rossi, *J'attendrai*, for me. Sentimental nonsense— but it belongs to where we're going.'

It was the first loosening that Kenworthy had observed in him. And Neville went on in relaxed mood:

'All right, Kenworthy. You've not been quite such a nuisance as it might seem. I'd hoped to be out of Nice by ten, but there's another bus at two. We can spend the morning fitting you out. Put it all down on your expense sheet. My wife can afford it. It will teach her a lesson. And don't let's misunderstand one another: I know that I'm on trial too. It's your privilege to decide whether I'm worth protecting—from whatever I might need protecting from.'

If only the bugger would laugh—

Neville organized Kenworthy's shopping. They packed their unwanted clothes and deposited their hand baggage in lockers at the bus station.

'With any luck we'll see that lot again in three weeks' time. Yes: three weeks should about do it. Snack lunch?'

With time to kill they wandered about the bus station's artificial terraces and saw there a sight which had them sharing a spontaneous thought. A young man—he would not be more than twenty-three—was half sitting, half lying, half asleep with a small dog half sleeping at his feet. His lank hair was shoulder length and his complexion was the legacy of hard drugs. In front of him stood a bowl containing a few odd francs and on the roughly torn edge of a cardboard carton he had scrawled an appeal:

MY DOG HAS NOT EATEN TODAY

Neither man paid open attention, but when they were scarcely more than half a pace past, Neville stopped and half turned.

'Kenworthy—that bugger's English.'

Kenworthy stopped too and looked. The man had a small Union Jack sewn into a corner of his lumber-shirt pocket. Neville swooped down on him, pulled him to his feet, thumped him once in the diaphragm, and when he was doubled, came up under his chin. The man fell back against the concrete rockery. The dog whimpered, trembled, and ran a few yards away.

'I feel better for that,' Neville said, adjusting the fit of his rucksack. 'A lot better.'

CHAPTER 4

At two o'clock they pulled out of the Gare Routière on an uncomfortably crowded bus. Kenworthy and Neville were sitting wedged together, Kenworthy on the window side.

'What's the bravest thing you ever did in your life, Kenworthy?'

The landscape was outer urban: vintage villas in terraced gardens; bougainvillæa and palms. Neville's question came so suddenly that an immediate answer was almost forced to be true.

'By brave, of course, I include bloody stupidity—some occasion when you put your life at risk, not because you believed in what you were doing, but because it was expected of you.'

'It depended on who was doing the expecting.'

'Those about you. The way they'd conditioned you. The System.'

Somehow one tried to give true answers to Neville.

'Northern France, after Falaise. I went over a level-crossing on a motorbike, under shellfire from a tank.'

'Why? Couldn't you have waited?'

'I had a meet on the other side.'

'Worth the risk, was it?'

'No. The meet didn't materialize.'

'Did anybody ever acknowledge that as brave?'

'No one ever knew. Things like that were going on all the time.'

'See what I mean? Bloody stupidity.'

'And you, Neville?'

'I jumped out of a captive balloon on my parachute course. Of all the jumps I ever made—only one operational —departing from that moored basket was the toughest I ever faced. Somehow, committing myself to the slipstream of an aircraft was nothing like as bad as leaving the safety of that basket. I suppose it was feeling umbilically bound to Mother Earth that was the trouble.'

They were finally beyond the city limits and climbing a grey valley that the developers already had their hands on: blocks of flats, still unfinished, but already placarded as luxuries.

'I'd done my best to persuade them I'd no need for practice jumps. I was going to do one operationally, and

one only. 1943. So let that be it, I argued. If I was going to
be killed, I'd be killed just once. Why flirt with death half
a dozen unnecessary times?'

'This was for SOE?'

Kenworthy tried to put it casually. Neville tended to
evade questions leading in that direction.

'Not *for* SOE. They organized my training, but I wasn't
one of their regulars. I never worked for them.'

They stopped in an ancient village. Many got out and
many got in. The air was recharged with garlic.

'I told you I came for a walking tour in Provence while I
was at the House: sorry—Sandhurst to you. With two
others, though I was the only one whose French was up to
much. The other two both made Major-General and one of
them thought of me when an assignment came up. He
remembered that I knew something of the area, that I wasn't
averse to the people. And he knew I could live on short
commons for a week or two if I had to.'

'So they dropped you in among this lot?'

Kenworthy indicated the wooded slopes, the inhospitable
terrain which, between contemporary building lots, was a
boulder-strewn glacial moraine. It was not country in which
there seemed to be much that a man could live off.

'No. Higher up. They did at least have the savvy to put
me down on a plateau.'

They had to lean against centrifugal force as they rounded
a hairpin.

'Need I say that it didn't come off? One of the silliest,
most idly thought out, most casually hypocritical schemes
that the mind of even military man has ever conceived. It
was wasteful of material and human lives. I came back, and
they never used me for anything like it again. I was put
back on making brilliant contributions to forward planning
that no one ever used. Now do you know?'

'I'd like to know more.'

'Maybe sometime I'll tell you. Maybe I won't.'

'Have you been in touch since—with those you worked with up here?'

Neville took time considering whether to reply.

'To give you a short answer, this is my first trip to France since the war ended. But I think that's enough about all that for now, Kenworthy.'

Kenworthy could not resist the feeling that Neville wanted to be more explicit; it was he, after all, who had brought the subject up. But there was something about the story that he could not bring himself to tell. They reached their terminus—a dusty hill village whose smells were aggressively different from those of the city: a mingling of baking bread, of North African tobacco, of street dust and dubious drains. If any of the small shops were open for business, they did not look it. Two small children took sightings on the alighting passengers with plastic submachine-guns. A dog woke, snapped at flies, then fell asleep again with the flies still pestering him.

Neville's behaviour was mildly peculiar. He looked about them in search of something that he was obviously unable to find—perhaps not in itself significant: places changed in forty years, memory made mistakes. He went to the back of the bus and studied the destination-board: St Cyr. When their driver had finished unloading packages, he went and asked him a question that Kenworthy could not hear. Then he came back looking thoughtful.

'I noticed a sign down the road, pointing the way to an official tourist camp site. I suggest we take advantage of it, since this is our first night out. We might as well get used to living without latrines by easy stages.'

It was only when the whole thing was over that Kenworthy discovered that Neville had brought them to the wrong place—and on the wrong bus. Neuvechapelle St Cyr, some seventeen kilometres north-west of here—that was where they should have gone. Neville said nothing about it. He was never good at admitting himself mistaken.

He sent Kenworthy to buy fresh bread, a hundred grammes of peasant *pâté* and a bottle of Côtes de Provence for their supper. For half an hour they talked absurd politics again, each in turn devil's advocate for some unlikely cause or other. It was difficult to know what Neville really believed. The subsequent night had its chills, and Kenworthy was awake for a full hour in deep blackness. Then he woke to a frosty dawn that made him glad to sink deeper into his sack for another half-hour. When he got up, he found Neville sitting on a stone, studying his map.

They struck their bivouacs and Neville led them up an unmade road that presently petered out into a mule-track round the rim of a col without apparent destination. For hours at a stretch they had no conversation. Neville called a halt, army fashion, for the last ten minutes in every two hours, and Kenworthy took stock of a landscape that was becoming more and more lunar: occasionally a view of an alp coned with unblemished snow, with here and there a pretentious villa belonging to someone who fancied this as country living. But the life of even a generation ago looked as if it had disappeared. There were centuries-old olive groves that had not been attended to for years, farmhouses in the old Provençale mode in ruins almost down to their foundations, the crumbled conduits of ancient irrigation systems.

'I take it we're making our way up to your plateau, Neville?'

'Feeling Blighty-minded already, Kenworthy?'

'I will when you do.'

'I'm cheating a bit. It will take us two days to get to where I landed: that was near a village called St Blaise des Figuiers. This is virgin territory even for me. But I've always wanted to look at this particular range on foot.'

Anything rather than admit that he had brought them to the wrong St Cyr . . .

They were climbing a ridge, along a track that wound

back and forth on itself, rousing the hope that every next
stretch would see them at the summit. But every next corner
was the beginning of a fresh rise. About the middle of the
afternoon, Kenworthy began to know how sadly he was out
of condition. Every muscle was beginning to shriek for rest.
Neville had got ahead of him, and in trying to increase his
pace, Kenworthy's cramps were becoming disastrous. At
length Neville waited for him. He too was breathing hard,
and for the first time Kenworthy noticed that he was in
some distress, though it was impossible to tell whether this
was due to the condition for which he needed surgery, or
whether he had merely overestimated his capacity for uphill
walking.

'Want to call it a day, Neville?'

'Oh-ho—feeling knocked up, are you. Kenworthy? Finding muscles you'd forgotten you had?'

'Not finding muscles—that's the trouble.'

Neville called a halt—ostensibly for Kenworthy's benefit
—and found a spot on a rocky platform where they could
pitch their tents. A clean and icily cold mountain rill plunged
down past them, and there was enough brushwood about
for them to start a fire. Neville cooked them a packet of
soup.

'All my life,' Neville said, 'I've wanted to retread Steven-
son's route through the Cévennes.'

'At least he had a donkey.'

'Not the least of his troubles.'

Sunset was a massive spread of red against a bank of
blue-black cloud. To Kenworthy's surprise, Neville produced a pipe and lit up. It was the only time he had
ever seen him smoke. The aroma was peculiar. Perhaps he
smoked a herbal mixture.

'Is it likely that there'll be many people left that you knew
forty years ago, Neville?'

'They aren't the only ones that interest me,' Neville said,
and left that enigma uninterpreted.

'You came to organize Resisters?'

Kenworthy was becoming skilled at spotting the moments when Neville seemed willing to talk.

'Not to organize them. I met quite a number—inevitably: a mixed bunch. There were almost as many motives for Resistance, you know, as there were participants. Sentimental patriotism, middle-of-the-road socialism, communism, revenge, the need to be part of a team for mutual support on the run—just think how many separate movements there were: *Combat, Libération, Francs-Tireurs*, the *MUR*, the *MLN* —the *National Front*, the *Conseil National de la Résistance*. You'll have read novels—'

'And seen films.'

'They mostly got it wrong,' Neville said. 'Where there's danger, there'll be romantic adventurers. But not all of them saw it through to the end. There were weaklings as well as strong men, and the line between Resistance and crime was not always finely drawn. Some men's way in was through the black market—and that didn't always bring out the noblest streak in them.'

None of which was news to Kenworthy—but it seemed best to let Neville lead himself.

'I'll introduce you to a few of them—perhaps. I don't know; I don't, as you say, know who's left—or where some of them will have got to. And not many of them were indigenous to this area.'

He started poking at the embers of their fire with a stick.

'We've nothing to fear tonight from lions and hyenas. There's no point in keeping this going. But let's have another last blaze.'

They scouted around for more fuel.

'I was dropped here to meet a German,' Neville said, quite suddenly.

'A German?'

'It seems a long way round to come and find one, I dare

say. What do you know about the German Resistance, Kenworthy?'

'That there effectively wasn't any—till certain elements in the army decided they had had enough of a corporal's strategy. Von Stauffenberg tried to get the Führer with a lethal briefcase.'

'I mean popular Resistance—the equivalent of all these French schoolteachers, railwaymen and small shopkeepers, who were ultimately getting their orders from London.'

'There weren't any,' Kenworthy said. 'The Nazis had been too crafty for them.'

'You believe that?'

'Look at it in cold blood. The Communists were liquidated as soon as the Brownshirts took power. Jewish money had been immobilized by the terror. Hundreds of thousands went to the concentration camps. All practical opposition had been dissolved.'

'And there was no one dissatisfied enough, mad enough, or so hungry for revenge that he'd try to take the Establishment on?'

'Look,' Kenworthy said. 'I remember a case I heard of in Hamburg. It happened as far back as 1937. The middle-aged father of a family shot off his mouth about the government one Saturday night in his local. That weekend was the last time his family saw him. A fortnight later his wife had a postcard saying that if she called at a given address, she could collect his ashes. That sort of thing didn't exactly encourage conspiracy.'

'There were French men and women who suffered no less.'

'Admitted. But they were *Occupied*. They were *in situ* and fighting back. They hadn't been liquidated in advance.'

'But weren't there Germans who didn't believe? Weren't there intelligent young soldiers occupying Paris who for the first time in their lives were catching glimpses of a culture that they'd been taught was decadent? Hadn't they started

to think that there might be a few worthwhile ideas in
Europe that they hadn't been taught in the *Hitler Jugend?*
And which of them wasn't dreading the order to take a train
from the Gare de l'Est—the first lap to the Eastern Front?'

'They weren't organized.'

'Wasn't there a time when the French weren't organized?
If there were men in Germany wanting to be organized—
couldn't we have helped? As we organized the French?
Wouldn't it have shortened the war?'

'It didn't happen.'

'And why didn't it happen? Could it possibly have been,
do you think, because the movement would have been so
left-wing that it wouldn't have been acceptable to some of
our top people? Wasn't that why Churchill tolerated de
Gaulle—so that *mon Général* could ride-a-cock-horse into
Paris in 1944 and belie the claim that it was only the
Communists who had fought back?'

'I was never a fan of de Gaulle,' Kenworthy said.

Twilight had taken a very short time to tighten its hold.
Already the red in the sky had reduced itself to a faint
narrow strip.

'So I was sent here to make contact with a German.'

'It seems a curious place to choose for the rendezvous.'

'Because it was as important to protect the German's
security as it was to protect mine. Perhaps even more so.'

'And what came of it?'

'Nothing.'

Neville tamped the bowl of his pipe and applied a fresh
match to it.

'That is—nothing as far as I ever knew. Not that I had
any right to expect to be told. No: I came home and they
put me back in an office to write hypothetical military papers
that nobody wanted to read. I'm more likely to find the real
answer up here than ever I was to hear it from the War
Office.'

'You've left it a long time,' Kenworthy said.

Neville flicked some tiny black insect off his knee.

'I'm a moral coward, that's why. I think I can say I was never a physical one.'

He got up and carefully knocked out his pipe against his hand, stamped on the ash, examined the empty bowl, tested it with the tip of a finger, then flung the briar far away from himself into the advancing shadows. They heard it ricochet from a rock.

'That's one of their conditions. That's one of the reasons I'm having to wait a month for a bed. The anæsthetist insists that I give up smoking.'

That was the only reference to his operation that he ever made. The next morning they went over the crest of the ridge they had been climbing for two days and started to come down its northern slope. Neville looked up at the gothic vaults of the conifers above them.

'I must have parachuted down over this lot. They'd allowed, of course, for the prevailing wind—and if there'd been an unexpected change in the weather pattern, God knows where I'd have landed. It was very different from my training drops. Then we had jumped as a *stick*, following each other fast out of the hatch. We were pre-empted by the order of our rings on the wire, and when one's turn came, one had no choice. I don't count as courage anything you do in a pack. That can be no more than herd foolishness. But when it came to the real thing, I had only the despatcher to impress. And he was an enigma with whom I'd made no progress: a turkey-faced flight-sergeant with a Glaswegian accent and the philosophy that my mission was none of his business. I remember when he started opening the hatch, I asked myself—only in theory, you'll understand—what would be the consequences if I refused to jump. He gave me a shove at the operative second. I suppose even in that moment of truth I'd no choice, philosophically speaking.'

They came to a forest edge over which they could look out across a stretch of plain—Neville's plateau—a patchwork of

arable fields, with occasional knots of trees unidentifiable at
this distance. At this stage they were skirting a sheer rock-
face some two hundred feet deep.

'Yes. I must have floated poetically down over all this
lot. What terrified me most was the blackness. There was
nothing to be seen—nothing anywhere. I'd been briefed
about a light pattern to look for, but I could see nothing at
all. They hadn't blacked-out up here: there were rare lights
to be made out as I came down through the cloud base: a
hamlet, a few isolated farms, a car on a road. But nothing
was where I'd expected it to be. I was going to miss my RV,
and the only thing to concentrate on was my landing—I'm
sorry, Kenworthy—you must be finding this a hell of a
bore.'

'In no way.'

'Bear with me. I came here to relive this, so forgive me
if I'm reliving it. If I were on my own, I'd probably be
talking to myself.'

They caught another glimpse of the plain. Two miles
away a service bus crept like a toy up a long shallow slope
between villages. The area into which they were coming
was remote, but—at least nowadays—it was not detached
from civilization.

'I narrowly missed an olive tree, then a whole bloody
grove of them, then came down in a field that we are going
to try to find again. I rolled over, got out of my harness and
kept dead quiet for a full half-hour. According to my briefing,
there would be a guide, somewhere. But he—or she, as it
turned out—had known as well as I did how likely this
stage was to abort. The master plan had not left us without
alternatives. And one of those alternatives was to use our
initiative.'

There was a notice nailed to a tree, warning that the
hunting in this part of the forest was private. Someone had
plugged the board with a salvo of shot.

'My first job was to get rid of that bloody parachute.

According to standing orders, I ought to have set about that within seconds of landing. But my mind was obsessed by the need not to show myself. My plane would have been heard. Its course would have been plotted. It had turned back. No bombs had been dropped, so its purpose would have been supposed. In my favour, German troops about here were thin on the ground. The Occupation had been extended to the whole of France after the landings in Tunisia in 1942, but they hadn't exactly flooded the stonier passes of Provence with field-grey soldiers. One was more likely to come across Italian military, as near as this to their own borders. And I don't know about you, Kenworthy—I never did take the Eyeties all that seriously. But I dare say that's being unfair to them. *Il Duce* must have had some marksmen who could have got me at point-blank range. But the worst danger came from the French, not from the Axis. Bassompierre's Milice was a Vichy police force at the service of the German army. They were eager to impress, which was why they were the bastards they were. There was even a French Gestapo, thugs like Henri Lafont, flat out to prove that Jacquot could do anything that Fritz could. Forget films and novels, Kenworthy. This wasn't a nation made up ninety per cent of patriots, all looking for opportunities for sabotage. Nor was collaboration a mere matter for Vichy. There were thousands at local level who were out for any advantage that they could wangle. Some just wanted to get on with their own lives: the selfish bastards. Moral principles can become expendable when your family's survival is on the line.'

They came across a couple of forestry workers blazing trees for felling. Neville shouted down to them through a clearing.

'Are we on the right track for St Blaise?'

'St Blaise des Figuiers? You can't get to St Blaise this way. There's a bridge down. You'll have to go round by Fresnes les Puits.'

'Fresnes les Puits,' Neville said, with a touch of drama
that he might possibly be overdoing. 'Kenworthy, how could
I ever have forgotten a place-name like that? I haven't
thought of Fresnes les Puits since I last kicked its dust from
my shoes. My God! When you speak of France, don't
mention Fresnes les Puits in the same breath.'

They had been talking easily for an hour, but Neville now
went into a silence. Kenworthy did not attempt to break it.

Then the Colonel abruptly decided that they had come
far enough for today, although it had been an unexacting
stretch, nearer to six miles than the twenty which were his
usual target. Again it was impossible to tell whether the
exertions of the day had been too much for his age, or
whether it was something deeper that was corroding him.
The spot he chose was not even a particularly favourable
one. There was no water-supply handy, and they had to
make do with a litre-sized bottle that he carried.

'We're bound to come across a stream lower down, first
thing in the morning.'

Kenworthy occupied himself with their fire. Neville chose
a position for his bivouac some distance from Kenworthy's
and after an unappetizing supper disappeared into it, showing no desire for their usual idiotic debate. Why was it that
they had drifted so naturally into talking the nonsense they
did? Each was taking it in turn to mock the slogans of Right
as well as Left. Was it because neither of them believed in
either side?

Kenworthy lost no time over extinguishing their fire,
which he did in the most primitive fashion that suggested
itself. Neville called good night to him as he was tying down
the flap of his bivouac. Clearly he was not minded to finish
the story of his landing. All because he had remembered a
village called Fresnes les Puits, where something had gone
catastrophically wrong?

In the morning, after Kenworthy had reminded himself
where he was, from the mingled smells of canvas and earth,

he crawled out among the trees and discovered that Neville had gone. There could be no doubt about his departure. The space where his tent had been pegged was as vacant as if he were miles away already.

CHAPTER 5

Neville had left him no message, no water, no breakfast—which did not matter all that much, since he was not really far from places where there were people. He would be able to deal with his peckishness within a couple of hours. Nor did he imagine that he would have much difficulty in picking up Neville's spoor, though that depended partly on the hour of night at which Neville had set out—and on how keenly he had bothered to try to cover his tracks. Kenworthy did not feel unduly distressed at his deception, nor was he greatly worried about how long it would take him to catch up with the Colonel. The old man had reached a crisis in his hunt for forgotten things. A day alone with his thoughts was his right—and, Kenworthy thought, perhaps as much as he'd be able to stand before he needed company again.

Kenworthy walked downhill for two hours and saw nothing but trees. He met not a solitary soul coming up or down. One tree bore an advertisement for an eating-house in St Blaise des Figuiers, but this had been assaulted by the elements and half its message obliterated. The sign might have been there since before the war.

An empty stomach was one thing; thirst was another, and after five miles he had a drought under his tongue that was beginning to make itself unpleasant. The first water he found was confined in a cavity of brown earth and stank of hydrogen sulphide.

Then he heard a running stream, and this was no mirage. He had come to a part of the wood where the only navigable

track ran along the rim of a ravine, and after half a kilometre
he reached the broken bridge of which yesterday's forester
had told them. Its collapse had been fundamental and there
was no hope at all of making a crossing. The chasm was
deep and its sides almost vertical. A practised climber would
undoubtedly have got fun out of it, but anyone but an
exhibitionist would have preferred to seek his fun securely
roped to a mate.

So Kenworthy had to forget about St Blaise. He had
better find his way to Fresnes les Puits, clearly the scene of
more than trivialities in Neville's experience. But Fresnes
les Puits meant nothing to Kenworthy. He and Neville had
saved expense by not duplicating their maps, but Neville
had clung possessively to his stock and Kenworthy had
nothing on a large enough scale to help with Provençale
villages. Since he could see no other track than the one
which led to the shattered bridge, there was nothing for it
but to retrace his steps.

Climbing again now, it took him more than two hours to
reach the spot where they had slept, and still there was no
alternative to continuing upwards. After another hour he
came to where the woodmen were working.

'St Blaise des Figuiers?'

One of them answered him in a regional *patois* of which
he could not grasp a word, but these were not men who
gave up readily. They were determined to transmit meaning
and by sheer will-power they did so. They directed him
down the slope, with knife-and-fork gestures that were the
most hopeful signs he had seen for some time. He slithered
down between the trees until he came to a tractor and
trailer, parked by a stack of sawn logs. Here they shared
their midday snack with him: crusty bread and chewy
sausage—and red wine, decidedly non-vintage, poured into
one's mouth from leather flasks of a pattern that had been
in use for centuries.

Had they seen his friend?

What friend?

Another Englishman who was walking through the forest. A man carrying a brilliant blue rucksack.

Oh, Kenworthy was English, was he? He spoke fine French for an Englishman.

Bullshit. But Kenworthy did not argue with them.

What sort of a man was he then, Kenworthy's friend?

'Grand. Fort.'

Kenworthy squared his shoulders and mimed a minor giant. This initiated prolonged debate, so copious with words and counter-words that something must surely result from it.

'Mais non, monsieur—'

What time had they come up here?

They had arrived at first light.

So Neville must have struck camp early in the night, perhaps as soon as he was sure that Kenworthy was asleep. These were dangerous tracks to walk at night, especially for a man who did not know them. Kenworthy asked how many ways led out of the forest.

There was the track direct to St Blaise, but it was closed. There was another track to Fresnes les Puits. That was the way they themselves would be going at the end of their day. They would take Kenworthy with them if he cared to wait for them. The only other path out of the trees was southwards, and it forked first two ways, then many more ways. If Kenworthy's friend had chosen that route, he would be a very difficult man to follow.

The sun was weary of the day before the foresters gave up work. Neither their trailer nor the tracks down which they drove it had been designed for passengers. At every corner Kenworthy had to wedge himself with bruised knees and chafed elbows. The vehicle had strong headlamps and he could see how the landscape was changing. They came to a slightly wider and better-surfaced track, which brought them into open scrub country. The road here had steep dips and rises. Presently they turned into a metalled highway, began to be overtaken by normal traffic. They entered the boundaries of the commune of Fresnes les Puits: a church, a dusty square lined with heavily pollarded limes and terraced for *la boule*, one or two dingy cafés. Did Kenworthy want to get out here? If not, they were going on to St Blaise.

He opted for that. They dropped into a valley, then climbed a long, slow hill, finally entering St Blaise under a fortified archway that all but had Kenworthy's hand off at the wrist. They put him down in a diminutive Place de la Libération.

St Blaise was a *village perché*, a village built on top of, and partially carved into, the bedrock. That had been for communal defence against raiding Saracens, probably, for although it had taken Kenworthy a long time to get here, it was not far from the sea as the crow flew. The Place itself was well kept, and had a plaque commemorating the hanging of one Jacques Vittorini, *Patriote*, in July, 1944. But apart from this neat and clean little square, the two striking impressions of St Blaise were that the place was medieval and deserted.

Normally the shops would still be open at this evening hour, but today being Monday, everything was closed. The bakery looked as if it had been boarded up for years. The outside stands of the all-purpose grocery were empty. The window of a fancy goods shop displayed stationery and ballpoint pens, but the bars across its door looked as if they had been brought as government surplus from some discontinued gaol.

In one corner, suspiciously dimly lit, was the Hôtel du Grand Rocher, but there was something about its exterior that would have repelled any traveller who was not in desperate straits. It had a large and very obviously hand-lettered placard proclaiming *Fermeture Annuelle*. Presumably its management was at this moment relaxing in Tenerife.

There were three café-taverns. One, an integral part of the Grand Rocher, looked as derelict as its mother institution. The Cercle was obviously though not aggressively closed. In the third, Les Tilleuls, there was light and Kenworthy heard the sound of men's voices raised. He pushed open the door and was dismayed to see that the chairs had already been lifted on to the tables. Only one table had been left undisturbed, and at this a dirtily dressed and sick-looking man was eating a plate of fried eggs. A stunted drudge, sweeping a mass of cigarette-ends and torn lottery tickets across the floor, did not hesitate to push her broom over Kenworthy's foot. Behind the bar a thickset and bellicose-looking man in his thirties was casting up the contents of the till and clearly did not care for his concentration to be disturbed. Kenworthy waited until he had reached a possibly accessible stage.

'Can I get something to eat here, please?'

'Tomorrow. We're closed.'

'I'm not asking for anything elaborate.'

'I'm sorry. There's no bread left. Closed, monsieur.'

'Well—is there anywhere in the village where I can get a bed for the night?'

'Have you tried across the road at the Grand Rocher?'

The man eating fried eggs looked at Kenworthy with watery and unconcerned eyes. There were kitchen noises behind a door marked *Privé*. The man behind the bar returned to his cashing up.

'The Grand Rocher is closed.'

Surely these people here knew that? The place was only opposite.

'Is there anywhere else with rooms to let?'

'*Ah, non.* This is not Nice or Cannes, monsieur.'

'Well, perhaps you can tell me this. Has any other Englishman been this way today?'

'Not to my knowledge, monsieur.'

The kitchen door opened, releasing aromas that had

Kenworthy salivating. A reasonably well turned-out woman came out and brought the sick old man his dessert—an unpeeled apple on a plate. She said something to the barman in *patois* and went back into the kitchen.

But Kenworthy had noticed something else while the kitchen door had been open. Among the mingled odours there was one which seemed strangely familiar—though he did not recognize it at once. Now he identified it. It was the tang, unique in his experience, of Neville's tobacco, as he had smoked it the other night before throwing away his pipe. Kenworthy wished the barman *à demain* with exaggerated formality and went out again into the Place without much hope of unearthing anything. He made a tour of St Blaise, but found nothing helpful. Every stone in the village seemed to date from the Middle Ages. It was probably true that every front door would open into a household splendid with the latest consumer durables. Every middle-class housewife in St Blaise would have her washing machine, every home a colour TV. There were high-powered Japanese motorcycles parked in many of the doorways. But there was nothing modern in the externals. The narrow streets wound up and down stone steps as they had done for centuries. It would be physically impossible to put up another building in the place. Every narrow-fronted house depended absolutely on its neighbour. How had they ever started to build here in the first instance?

The village was surprisingly well lit, with bulbs set in mock-archaic lanterns designed to suit the décor. Yet an imaginative man might sense a sort of historic evil about the place. Behind these walls lived a modern community. But this stonework had witnessed religious intolerance, political intransigence, poverty, cruelty and despair. The ancient iron grilles over the windows had seen violent death. The asymmetrical doorways, the overhanging alcoves and balconies had been the backcloth to every possible permutation of human deception and treachery.

And this was not fanciful. It was Kenworthy's accumulated policeman's experience as he walked the honeycomb of deceptively squalid-seeming streets. St Blaise seemed unpopulated—but behind its walls were living people. There were eyes behind the louvres and shutters, curtains that would be opened a fraction of an inch to see whose footsteps had passed.

And Neville was somewhere in St Blaise, had been here most of today. Neville had warned St Blaise that Kenworthy would be coming. Neville had smoked a pipe in Les Tilleuls —he must presumably be carrying a spare. He was probably staying at the inn. Kenworthy's reception had been staged under his orders.

Kenworthy knew that he had behaved lackadaisically in everything he had touched in this case so far. Now he was at a moment of decision: stay with it or leave it.

Every instinct said stay not too far away from Neville. The first thing now was to move himself and get things into his control.

CHAPTER 6

Flou: that was the word the French had for it—flaccid, pudding-brained; without direction—*papillotant*—fluttering whimsically from one under-exposed impression to the next. That was how Kenworthy had been conducting himself. All because of Neville. All because he had let this sick old man call all the tunes.

Kenworthy did not know whether Neville deserved any man's respect or not. Neville had chosen to shove him off the *piste*—and his commission from Neville's wife had been to stay on the *piste*. Therefore he was going to get back on the track, he was going to stay on it as best he could, make his mind up about nothing until he had all the evidence.

And if he never did succeed in finding it, he did not have to let that trouble him either.

He walked the mediæval alleys of St Blaise until he was sure he must have passed along every one of them four times. He mastered the outline of the village, whose design and purpose, it seemed, was to rise up on all sides to the ramparts of a small modernized fortification that appeared to be privately occupied. From here the village fell in every direction to what had clearly been its original outer defences, or perhaps a more recent attempt to reconstruct them.

For the fourth time he passed a door that he studied more intently than most of the others. It looked a small house—though it was difficult in St Blaise to be sure quite what constituted a house. So many streets were no more than narrow flights of stone steps, and often someone's street entrance was on top of someone else's fifth floor. This house was set back about a metre and a half in an alcove on one of the descents. Its ground-floor windows were protected by heavy grilles and its door sported a brass plate that bore witness to several decades' weathering.

PAUL C. AUBIN
Docteur de Médecine
Faculté de Montpellier

After his fourth inspection, Kenworthy did not hesitate to set Dr Aubin's manually operated bells in motion. He had to find his way into the nervous system of St Blaise, and five minutes' conversation with a professional man of standing might possibly yield something.

The walls were so thick that it was impossible to tell from outside whether the bell-pull had activated anything. Kenworthy was about to try for a second time when the door opened. A woman, well-rounded but short of stature, stood looking out at him with distrust. She was wearing a grey habit and a dark blue headdress that might have been the uniform of a religious order. But Kenworthy—who did not know a great deal about religious orders—thought that perhaps this was a woman who simply preferred to affect the discipline and image of such a society: as if she belonged to a one-woman order of her own devising and direction. He noticed that despite the costume, she wore no religious insignia: no crucifix, no rosary. He took her to be the housekeeper-receptionist, and she looked the type to have her master under a fiercely protective wing. Her eyes conveyed to Kenworthy that if he were to get through this front door, it would be against the last expended shred of her will. And in case her will were not enough, she kept the door on the chain.

'Monsieur?'

'I wanted to ask—this is a private visit, not a professional one—I wanted to ask for five minutes of Monsieur le Docteur's time. Is he at home?'

'He is dining with friends at Draguignan. I do not expect him back before midnight. If it is an urgent medical problem, I can give you the telephone number of a doctor in Fresnes les Puits.'

'No, it is not a medical problem—or let's say at least that it could be, but I hope it isn't. I'm sorry if I'm talking in riddles. I have been on a walking tour with a friend, you see, another Englishman who is basically a very sick man. Due to stupidity over reading a map, I have become parted from him. But St Blaise was to have been the next stage of our journey, and I wondered if he might have arrived here before me. I thought perhaps he might have called here to replenish his stock of drugs.'

'There has been no Englishman here since last autumn.'

'You haven't heard whether one has arrived in the village today?'

'How would I have heard? I have not been out since I went for the morning bread.'

She was as hostile as the atmosphere in Les Tilleuls.

'Ah, well, I'm sorry I've troubled you. It seemed the obvious thing, to ask the local medical man.'

She was clearly very ready to close the door on him.

'I don't suppose you could direct me to somewhere in St Blaise where I might find a night's lodging?' he said. 'Since your only hotel is closed?'

'This is not a tourist agency, monsieur.'

'No. I'm sorry I presumed to ask for neighbourly advice.'

He rasped that at her. He might as well start rasping at people, since it was the only treatment he was getting from anyone here. His sharp tone seemed to give her second thoughts about her attitude. Perhaps in the distant past she had had a refined upbringing, and he had reminded her of it.

'I don't know of anyone in the village who takes in tourists at this time of the year,' she said.

'I've been sleeping under canvas,' he told her. 'And at my age that has lost its charms.'

'Your only hope is in Fresnes les Puits. There is an *auberge* there—the Auberge des Platanes—Madame Piquemal. Many such places are not open at this time of the year, but I don't think the Platanes is closed. I don't think she dare turn away business at Les Platanes.'

'Thank you very much, madame.'

His renewed politeness seemed to affect her. To his surprise, she did not immediately edge him away into the street.

'Your English friend, too—it is even possible that you will find him at Fresnes. I do not think it is a village he would choose to go to—but there is hardly anywhere else in the locality where a stranger could put up at this time of year. In the meanwhile, if he does come here for Dr Aubin's help, it might be useful for us to be able to get in touch with you.'

She was looking at him, he thought, with a greater degree of curiosity than she had shown up to now. He could not make up his mind whether there was anything personal in her hint that Neville might not care to go to Fresnes. He was not even sure that it was a hint.

'Perhaps you would let me have your name and your friend's. Perhaps you might care to telephone some time tomorrow. Your friend is a man of your age?'

'Older,' Kenworthy said. 'Though you might not think so, to see us on the road. He certainly does not make me feel his junior.'

'Describe him to me.'

It sounded more like an order than a request. She was evidently a woman accustomed to sending people hither and thither.

'A big man, half a head taller than me. He has the appearance of what he is—a retired British army officer.'

'*Celui.*'

That one. It was difficult to analyse her tone. It revealed that she knew Neville—or knew of him. But what was her attitude? Distaste? Regret? Resignation to the inevitable—to the regrettably inevitable?

'You know him?'

Kenworthy heard the hopefulness in his own voice. But she did her best to withdraw the impression that his description of Neville had meant anything to her.

'No, monsieur. I was thinking of quite a different man.'

'A man who was here in the war years? An Englishman?'

'Monsieur—it would be better for you to come back tomorrow and talk to Dr Aubin.'

'You think that Dr Aubin will definitely be able to tell me something?'

'I think, sir, that you must speak to Monsieur le Docteur yourself.'

And then, as he was wishing her good night, she found it desirable to give him further advice.

'Believe me, sir—I would not send you to Les Platanes if I knew of anywhere else. But you'll be safe and comfortable there—though I would not, if I were you, be inclined

to discuss private business with the landlady. Madame
Piquemal—'

She appeared to dry up.

'Yes?'

'Please understand—I am nor criticizing Madame
Piquemal. She is not to be blamed for what once went on
under her roof. But she talks too much—as I am doing—'

She closed the door, as if she had become afraid of him
again. He walked round to the village garage to see if he
could get a taxi into Fresnes les Puits. But the forecourt was
as empty as if the place had gone out of business. There
were no lights on the pumps, no sign of life about the
residential quarters. Maybe the proprietor was also out
dining. So it had to be another long, hard slog. The Route
de Fresnes was not a long one, but it was steep, down into
a valley-bottom, then out of it again, along a road that made
few departures from the contours of its parent rock. In places
the upward gradient must have been one in five. Like St
Blaise, Fresnes les Puits was mounted on a pinnacle, but
less tightly, and with fewer inner convolutions. Fresnes had
a broader summit, a flatter central area, and it was on the
edge of this that he found the Auberge des Platanes: another
port of call apparently unoccupied. The bell-push evoked
no response. No lights were switched on. There was now a
chill in the evening that reminded him that he was fifteen
hundred feet above sea-level. A night in his bivouac became
less inviting with every half-hour that passed, but he had
just concluded that it was going to be unavoidable when life
appeared. It took the form of a tall, middle-aged lady
of spare frame and uncomfortable movements who was
nevertheless heavily made up in shades in which puce
predominated. Her raven-black hair was iridescent with
dye, and if she had carried a candle in one hand, with a
shotgun under her other arm, neither would have looked
out of place.

She had trouble manipulating the bolts, and she too kept

the door on the chain. Clearly she did not like the look of
Kenworthy at all. Hoteliers hereabouts, it seemed, were
reluctant to trust those who stood lawfully in front of them.
She seemed by no means certain whether she had a room
free for the night, though to judge from the keys on the
board in the cubby-hole, there was no guest on the premises.
Kenworthy let her see his eye resting on them. She licked
thin lips.

'Most of my rooms are being decorated and rewired.
There is—let me see—there is number five.'

She quoted him a price and looked as if she hoped it was
high enough to make him go away.

But Kenworthy smiled at her—which seemed to add
greatly to her suspicions. But she eventually sighed, reached
up for a key, and took him in a very ancient hydraulic lift
to a stale-smelling bedroom with wallpaper embossed with
gold escutcheons against a background of shocking purple.

The morning brought an inexplicable contrast. When he
came down to breakfast, Madame Piquemal smiled as if he
were a forgotten friend. Perhaps it was because he had not
raped her in the night. Perhaps it was because the cutlery
and removable fittings were still on the premises? Perhaps
it was even because he was still here himself. In a pleasant
conservatory she served him with *café au lait* and rolls still
warm from the baker's. After a moment of indecision, she
even brought him a jar of her homemade pumpkin jam,
which, she said, and he did not doubt it, was superior to the
caterer's stuff in the little foil containers.

A quarter of an hour later she came back to see if there
was anything else that he wanted, and to bring him a
newspaper. As he did not immediately pick this up, she
leaned over the table and began to read it herself, to the
accompaniment of a repertoire of clucks, clicks, hisses and
general disgust: the condition of the world this morning was
pretty much as usual, editorial ingenuity squeezing crises
out of ministerial prevarications, coalitions of terrorists,

militant pacifists and discontented labourers the world over.

Kenworthy grasped the opportunity and professed his own abhorrence of the state of society. She pointed with a heavily ringed finger at one particular item, something distinctly local about corrupt public supply contracts in the canton.

'It's the same at home,' Kenworthy said.

'Ah, no—here in France it is a way of life.'

'I suppose you have your special difficulties. When one thinks what your country has undergone this century—'

'And who has led us into all of that? *Les Français*—'

'But your nation has had so much to confuse it. What was brave and patriotic in wartime became anti-social when peace was declared. Old habits die hard.'

Madame Piquemal nodded knowingly, with tight lips.

'I'm thinking of your Resistance Movement,' he said, arrived at last. 'I've always heard that they were pretty strong hereabouts.'

'Here in Fresnes?'

The idea seemed to strike her as a kind of fantasy.

'I was thinking of the region in general.'

'In Fresnes you will find plenty of *anciens* resisters. They grew up like ergot on damp rye several hours before the last Boche left French soil.'

'I know. *Septembristes*, you called them, didn't you? No: I was thinking of the real underground.'

'Here in Fresnes?'

It seemed to be the least thinkable notion that had come to her ears for a long time.

'Surely the hills and scrub round here were just what the Maquis needed?' he suggested.

'The Maquis? You mean the Communists? Or those who took orders from a general in London whom none of us had ever heard of?'

'I mean those who had good reason to go into hiding. I mean the network of messengers, carriers of food, guides—'

'Who put the rest of the population in jeopardy with their antics.'

'I think you are being unfair, madame.'

'Of course I am. I am French. What fun is there in being fair? There would have been a good deal less suffering if things had been better organized.'

'I don't think they did all that badly. There were giants among them, when the truth came to be told.'

'Truth?'

'I'm not saying that all's been made known yet—'

'Nor ever will be—'

'You can't reject all the legends,' Kenworthy said. 'Where would I go, do you think, for a reliable account of what went on in this locality?'

'Not to anyone in Fresnes.'

'And in St Blaise?'

She looked at him as if all her suspicions of last night might suddenly return. But the cloud cleared—as if she were positively struggling to make light of it.

'You have reason to be interested in St Blaise?'

'I've heard people speak of the place in this context.'

'One hears stories,' she said. 'There's bad blood still.'

She looked at him hard, wondering whether to say more.

'You were connected with all that, monsieur?'

'I had a friend who was. I never did find out what actually happened to him.'

'In these parts?'

'In the neighbourhood of St Blaise.'

She chewed this over—apparently to a conclusion reluctantly but firmly reached.

'There are people I could send you to who might be able to tell you. Some of them don't like talking about it: and they're the best ones to go to. You won't hear the same tale from everyone—but you can put things together for yourself. The only true heroes are those who keep quiet about it.'

'Who, for example? Who could I talk to?'

'Let me make my own inquiries first.'

Meaning that she had to get people's permission before she passed him on to them.

'I'm not here for very long,' he said.

'You'll be coming back this evening? I'm certain to have something for you by then. I suppose it's Le Baou you want to know about.'

'Le Baou?'

'A word from the old language of Provence. It means a rock—a rocky hill on the other side of St Blaise. It goes back centuries. That was where St Blaise des Figuiers originally was—that's where the settlement started. But when they were struck by the Plague they moved everything and everyone, lock, stock and barrel. They abandoned Le Baou, because it was infected. They built themselves a new village, on the bare rock that they'd been looking across to for generations. There aren't many houses in St Blaise less than three hundred years old. Four hundred's nearer the mark.'

'So Le Baou is a national monument now, I suppose?'

'Twenty miles from here you wouldn't find many people who've even heard of it. There's not much to see there: a hillside, overgrown. The old hovels collapsed into their own foundations. People carted stone away to use in their own buildings. I dare say the place means something to archæologists. There isn't much for ordinary folk to look at.'

'And the wartime connection?'

'You were talking about the Maquis—the real ones—those who had to go to ground when Pierre Laval was shipping French labour to Germany, in exchange for our prisoners of war. Le Baou was one of their hide-outs. Some of them stayed there for months, even years, burrowed into the old ruins.'

'The Germans never raided the place?'

'There weren't many Germans about here. And Le Baou had advantages. The lookouts had long warning of any approach. There were no roads up it that a motor could use. When they attacked Le Baou—as they did once or twice—it had to be with tracked vehicles. The people on the hill knew they were coming before they left the road. The original folk of Le Baou had chosen a safe home for themselves. That held good in modern times too. When the Germans did climb Le Baou, they found no one there. They'd all scattered into the brush. The Boches confiscated anything worth having that they found and set fire to the rest. They did that more than once. At one time they even set up a permanent guard there, but took it away again when they needed manpower somewhere else.'

'So Le Baou must have been a key-point. It would be the report centre for anyone with legitimate reasons to contact this group?'

'I suppose that's how it would be.'

'A committee centre.'

'Probably. But you must remember, Mr Kenworthy, I had nothing to do with any of this. We kept ourselves closely quiet as a family. It was the only safe way. I am only repeating what I have heard.'

'And what is now common knowledge.'

'Wait till this evening, monsieur. I will find someone who will tell you chapter and verse.'

'Yes: but what I am wanting, you see, is to save myself time. Someone must have been in charge of Le Baou.'

She smiled, not far short of laughing.

'If you ask who that was, you might get more than one answer. There were times when more than one person reckoned to be in charge of Le Baou.'

Then her phone rang, and she went to it. Kenworthy charged his post-breakfast pipe and picked up the newspaper. There was nothing in it that greatly interested him. The editor did not seem to know of the existence of the United Kingdom.

CHAPTER 7

The phone call was for Kenworthy. Madame Piquemal called him. A woman announced herself.

'Madame Ripault. At Dr Aubin's. Monsieur Kenworthy, it is important that you should come here at once.'

'I'll do that.'

'It is also important that no one should see you come into St Blaise.'

What was the French for a cloak of invisibility?

'Monsieur Kenworthy, please listen carefully to what I say. Go to the hospital on the road that leads from Fresnes les Puits to Tanguy. Ask there for Dr Auguste Boillot. He will tell you what to do. There's a hospital van that will be coming to St Blaise in the middle of the morning. They will bring you here in it.'

Madame Piquemal had gone into her office and was looking through a handful of bills and bank statements. Obviously she had not missed a word that had been said at Kenworthy's end of the line.

'If I am not mistaken, that was the one who guards Dr Aubin's surgery.

'That is so.'

'The Lioness. Just don't take too much notice of anything she says, that's all.'

To judge from the blood-spattered overall coat that he was wearing, Dr Boillot at the hospital had had to be called away from a surgical operation. If one's first requirement in a doctor was his bedside manner, then one's preliminary search for promise in Auguste Boillot's appearance was likely to be disconcerting. He was a man of about Kenworthy's age, short, dark and thickset, with a heavy brow, a barrel chest and markedly rounded shoulders: a sub-tribal type that Kenworthy had already encountered a number of times in Provence.

But the moment he opened his mouth, his voice, which was surprisingly high-pitched, proclaimed him to be a patient, courteous and quick-witted man. He was perhaps a little too anxious to show off his English—which was embarrassingly limited—but otherwise was rather like a thoroughly amiable gorilla.

'So Marguerite Ripault has sent you to me?'

'If that is her name. Dr Aubin's receptionist—'

'Dear Marguerite. And you are connected in some way with this large man who was parachuted down near St Blaise in 1943?'

'Yes. I am his companion—and guardian, in so far as he will allow himself to be guarded.'

Boillot smiled. Kenworthy could not avoid the impression that Boillot knew a great deal about Neville—and that his impressions were likely to be worth hearing. But Boillot was clearly also in a hurry.

'You must forgive me. I have a patient who by now will be shivering with cold. You want to get to St Blaise—secretly?'

'Madame Ripault seemed to set great store by the secrecy.'

Boillot grinned and sent him with a porter to the driver of a little white van, painted *Service Hospitalier*. This driver was clearly in no hurry to go to St Blaise. It was an hour before they left, and Kenworthy had to help to load the van with cardboard cartons of surgical gloves, plastic syringes and disposable kidney bowls. Then he was bidden to make a nest for himself in the middle of these unupholstered packages. The ride could not have been less of a luxury in an unsprung eighteenth-century diligence. It became obvious after the first quarter of an hour that they were not going direct to St Blaise. They went up and down a switchback of secondary roads. They travelled over ruts and at one stage, apparently, over strewn half-bricks. They did sudden, fast turns in loose gravel; in addition to which, there seemed every danger of carbon monoxide poisoning from a perforated exhaust.

Kenworthy's interpretation of sound and movement told him when they arrived at last in a built-up area. They crawled over urban cobbles. A heavy metal object struck the side of the van. The nearside front wheel mounted a pavement, followed by its rear fellow. Then both wheels thumped back into the road. They stopped. The driver called to him not to get out until he was told to, and started unloading the cartons. They were outside Dr Aubin's, and the boxes were being put down on the pavement in such a way that he would be sheltered behind them as he walked in at the door.

Madame Ripault, in her nun's habit, was beckoning him with gestures of secrecy so urgent that she appeared to be angry with him. She ushered him across the entrance hall as if she had been sweeping him in with a broom. A woman patient with a child in her arms came out of one room and went into another. Madame Ripault twisted him by one shoulder, as if to minimize the likelihood that this woman should see his face. She thrust him through a door. He found himself in a long, narrow stockroom, on each side of which racks were lined with urinal bottles, bedpans and rubber tubing. He sat down on a stool and studied the saints' days on a promotional calendar pinned to the wall. It was some ten minutes before Madame came in, bringing coffee.

'You were lucky, Mr Kenworthy—I don't think you were seen.'

'I wouldn't expect tighter security if I'd been sent to abstract Lenin from his tomb.'

She did not look as if facetiousness appealed to her.

'It's never any use doing things by halves. It was as often as not only a careless second that brought people to Dachau or Buchenwald. I sent for you because I have news of the man you are interested in.'

Should Kenworthy tell her that he had smelled Neville's pipe tobacco?

'He has been and gone again,' Madame Ripault said.

'You know where he has gone?'

'That is something you'll be wanting to find out. That's why I got you here unbeknown to anyone in the village. You will not want to lose the element of surprise.'

She touched her lips with a forefinger. Had this woman done clandestine work during the tormented years—or was this simply how she thought one had to set about it? She looked at him, trying to convey a battery of emotive information: a shared understanding of the complexities of human behaviour.

'This man's arrival in 1943 was bad news for St Blaise. I am surprised that he has come back here. It might have been a little less surprising if he had come in, say, 1946 or '47.'

'But there must be someone here who will have made him welcome.'

'As to that—'

She frowned and shook her head as if she were sure that that was the best way of ensuring subtle thought-transference.

'It remains to be seen whether he has left of his own free will, or whether—'

She paused, and drew the edge of her extended fingers across her throat. Now Kenworthy knew that whatever else she was, she was first and foremost a ham actress. She might be in a position to help him—but any help that materialized would have to wait for all the stage business that she had ever learned. She was an over-dramatizer, an enjoyer of the suspense that she created. But the indications were that there would be something worth waiting for at the end of the build-up.

'You mean,' Kenworthy said, 'that everyone in St Blaise des Figuiers was in the same mind about Colonel Neville?'

'Is that really his name?'

'What is he known as here?'

'That depends on who you are. Some called him *notre petit voisin*—our little neighbour. Because he was no dwarf, you see. Others called him—'

'Yes?'

But Madame Ripault, who must have spent most of her life interpreting slight distant sounds, stopped talking to listen.

'Ah. The Doctor has finished with Madame Berry. You didn't hear anyone else go in, did you?'

She went out of the room, peeping melodramatically both ways along the corridor before entrusting herself to it. Ten seconds later she was back.

'Dr Aubin has no more patients. He'll be glad to talk to you. He always likes a few minutes' change of interest before he goes out on his round.'

Kenworthy was amazed at the modernity of Dr Aubin's consulting-room. All his equipment, his colour-matched cabinets and shelves, his sinks, his scales and his desk looked as if they had been ordered from this year's catalogue: this behind the mediæval walls of St Blaise. Kenworthy had rather expected him to be the sort of bearded old gentleman in a huge melon hat whom one pictured in the 1920s, strolling towards an apéritif through the Jardins du Luxembourg. The character waiting for him was a man in his early sixties, sparsely built, and totally in white from the tips of a tight-fitting skull-cap to the hem of his trimly belted coat, which buttoned at the throat like a caftan. There was something of both the god and the monkey about Dr Aubin. He gave the appearance of dispensing wisdom more importantly than pharmacy, of waiting for his next supplicant as if it were imperial judgement that he was distributing, rather than antibiotics and barbiturates.

And yet there was a latent agility about the man, an economy of movement, an impression of accrued knowledge that he had not allowed to fray at the corners. And though his eyes might convince a patient that he was being taken seriously, they had a readiness to laugh at what other men had not yet seen was ridiculous. Kenworthy soon got to know his cheese-slicing manner of setting nonsense at nought with one incisive, sardonic comment.

He motioned Kenworthy to a chair.

'Our other Englishman. I take it that Madame Ripault has put you in the picture?'

'I would hardly go as far as that, sir. But she has persuaded me that there is a picture.'

'Ah—she likes to build things up.'

Aubin had probably worked with Madame Ripault at his elbow throughout his professional career, might have inherited her from his father—had been kept at high-pressure efficiency by her. He knew how to by-pass her idiosyncrasies.

'Well—at least she got you here this morning.'

'With meticulous precautions,' Kenworthy said. 'I suppose I must count myself lucky that I was not actually carried in in a carton.'

'What do you mean?'

Kenworthy described with mock ruefulness the manner of his coming.

'Oh my God! She'd conduct my life like that too, if I'd let her. How does she think you are going to make inquiries in St Blaise without appearing to be here? Tell me, Mr Kenworthy—what is your relationship with *notre petit voisin*? You worked with him during the war, I take it?'

'No. Not at all.'

Kenworthy had to trust someone, and there was a hint of bright honesty about Aubin that might well be genuine. Briefly, and without dissimulation, he told him how he came

to be on Neville's heels. Aubin did not ask questions and
did not need to be told anything twice.

'Well, it seems to me,' he said, 'that your job here is going
to be tricky. There are mysteries connected with *notre petit
voisin* that no one has solved. You will understand that I
have never met the man. I am speaking of him as an
abstraction—as a figure in local history. He was bad news
for St Blaise from the moment he landed. I'm sorry to have
to say that, but it's true.'

'That is precisely the phrase that Madame Ripault used.'

Dr Aubin laughed lightly.

'What would you expect? She does her best to shape every
whisper of this throne. Small wonder if I talk like her.' He
extended his hands in the manner of a man about to count
out points.

'Would you like to hear the catalogue of disasters that
followed in the wake of your Colonel friend?'

Kenworthy did his best to preserve an expression of
neutrality, did not allow himself to show a trait of surprise.

'Item Number One: he landed as awkwardly as a raw
recruit, sprained an ankle. By his own admission he had
ignored the most elementary lessons he had learned in the
military gymnasium. He could barely get to his feet and was
unable to walk without support. He could not go forward
to meet his guide, so he sought shelter in a house—the worst
of possible houses, where he missed arrest by seconds. That
he was rescued at all was a matter of coincidences. He was
a man of extraordinary good luck, even if he did bring
misfortunes showering over others. His pilots spirited him
from under the nose-shadows of the *gendarmerie*. They somehow got him to Le Baou. They got a doctor to him.'

Aubin raised his eyebrows, hastening to correct Kenworthy's first thought.

'Not me. I was on the run from Montpellier at the time.
I was a medical student, and therefore considered capable
of making myself useful in the wilds—but not in this region.

I was doing what I could with minimal drugs for sick
Maquis in the Franche-Comté. *Notre voisin* had to rest his
ankle—at the very time when he ought to have been at his
most mobile. The doctor concerned was old Bézin. He put
notre petit voisin in plaster. A splendid type: qualified in
Toulouse in the 1890s. Didn't believe that the Germans
would not respect his Hippocratic oath. When they were
mopping up after your friend's departure, the Gestapo un-
earthed the Bézin connection. They took him from his
morning surgery—but the old man was crafty enough to
die of a self-inflicted prescription. And the cell, the chapel,
call it what you will, that had been saddled with the reception of your Colonel had to go out of existence. For three
months the Germans kept patrols on Le Baou—which made
things awkward for the St Blaise underground, because Le
Baou was essential to their strategy. Your Colonel did
nothing to advance the course of the war. I suppose you
know why they sent him here? It wasn't worth the aviation
fuel, the pilot's time, the parachute-packer's time or the
ground staff's time. And yet they put at risk an aircraft and
its crew. Your Colonel blew two transit routes, neither of
which our people here were ever able to use again. Six good
Frenchmen lost their lives because of him—the reprisals for
his visit were still going on when the final Boche retreat
started. When you're in the Place de la Libération, have a
look at the plaque to Joseph Vittorini. And Little Neighbour
was finally smuggled out of Menton by trawler, delivered
by dinghy to the conning-tower of a submarine somewhere
at sea. On its way home, the trawler was apprehended, the
crew arrested, eventually shot. The boat, their family's only
capital, was confiscated. And all so that your Colonel could
come and parley with a German.'

'He did begin to tell me about that—'

'If it was necessary for him to meet a German, why bring
the pair of them here? Why not arrange the meeting in the
Nord, where Germans were thirty for a sou? Why not in the

North-East, within pissing distance of the Fatherland? Why bring him down into sensitive territory like this?'

The surgery with its bits and pieces, its thermometers, spatulas, sphygmo-manometers, stethoscopes and paper-clips seemed irrelevant to all this—trivial against the forty-year-old tale of disaster. Scornful as he was, Dr Aubin remained unexcited, watching Kenworthy's face with keen interest.

'And why bring Chantal Dupuy here—to compromise her and worse.'

'Chantal Dupuy?'

A tremor of Aubin's lower lip suggested that he had come near to gasping.

'You have not heard of Chantal Dupuy? You do not know that last week Chantal Dupuy came back to St Blaise for the first time since those days? That—as far as I know—she is still here.'

'It is the first time I have heard her name.'

Dr Aubin did gasp.

'It sounds to me, Mr Kenworthy, as if you have come into this as badly briefed as your friend was when he dropped from the sky in October, 1943.'

'Even worse, I imagine.'

Aubin drew deep breath to force patience on himself.

'And yet you English win your wars. Chantal Dupuy is a national heroine. Chantal Dupuy was made a Commander of the *Légion d'Honneur,* holds the *Croix de Guerre* with stars and palm and the *Médaille de la Résistance.* She avoided limelight in the immediate post-war years, only to re-emerge in the upper reaches of the legal profession. For the last quarter of a century she has been a state prosecutor in the *Parquet* at Nantes. There are stories of innocent men who have pleaded guilty when they knew that she was briefed against them. And for the last week she has been staying in St Blaise. Up at the château.'

'Yes—I noticed the château last night.'

'The home of Jean-Paul Arribat, a retired judge.'

'And Madame—Mademoiselle?—Dupuy—was an active *Résistante* in the St Blaise area?'

'No. That is another part of the nonsense of it. She had been active in Brittany, and it was not until *l'affaire du petit voisin* that some unseen power drafted her here to Provence, to work with your Colonel—though why that was necessary, no one in this village has ever been able to fathom. I will tell you two stories about Chantal Dupuy. While she was active in this district, it became necessary to get supplies up to some characters who were dug in on a small-holding on the Montagne des Louves. It so happened that the *département* was being turned inside out in an anti-black-market drive, and to be caught carrying meat about was a one-way ticket. But Chantal Dupuy got fresh beef to her charges. She got it to them on the hoof, driving two beasts along main roads, looking like a farm girl, and actually flirting with the sentries on two German road-blocks.'

Dr Aubin sat back, enjoying Kenworthy's attention.

'The second case was something less of a gesture of bravado. One of the Vittorini family—Guillaume—came under Boche suspicion for having harboured your Colonel: a brother of the one who was ultimately hanged. He was arrested and taken in for questioning while your Colonel was still here. But while the Gestapo had him on the road, someone shot him from behind cover. A lot of people still believe that it was Chantal Dupuy who pulled that trigger. Everyone in St Blaise knew that Guillaume was likely to give way under torture: he was unlike his brother. And whether you believe that story or not—whichever way you judge Chantal Dupuy—you have to give her top marks for moral guts. It was said of her that she'd murder a man or sleep with him, according to which way she sniffed the battle-wind. And you've heard none of this?'

'No. If we'd had another week together, Neville might have told me all manner of things. He was struggling to unburden himself, but couldn't quite screw himself up to it.'

'I can understand his reluctance. Chantal was lucky to be able to salvage her career at law. Medals, stars and palms weren't her only legacy from Provence.'

Dr Aubin was skilled at evoking dramatic emphasis from pauses. He and Madame Ripault telling stories to each other would have made a fascinating act.

'You mean she fell into the biological trap?' Kenworthy asked.

'If you like to use phrases as coy as that. She had a child.'

'Of which Neville was the father?'

'That is the assumption in St Blaise. But it would be a wry world if everything that St Blaise assumed proved true. Neville may have thought so. For all I know, he may indeed have been. Opinion was divided among those who were in the best positions to have known. Those with a taste for strong drama said the child was Guillaume Vittorini's. The less charitable had it that Chantal Dupuy could not possibly have known for certain. So you see, Mr Kenworthy, there are things in St Blaise that are going to interest you.'

CHAPTER 8

Dr Aubin showed Kenworthy to the street door and Madame Ripault appeared from her sanctuary with an expression of professional self-effacement. She must surely be trembling at the rashness of allowing him to walk out into broad daylight. But ultimate obedience to the sudden whims of a mad master must be strongly embedded in her soul. She resisted the temptation to comment.

Kenworthy stepped into the narrow street, momentarily surprised by the warmth in the air and the babble of mid-morning life in St Blaise. The contrast with yesterday evening was hard to believe. This was a busy modern village, despite the age of its masonry. An electrician's van was attempting a wildly inadvisable manœuvre with three wheels on the pavement. Even the Café des Tilleuls had a colourful and active look. Metal tables with orange and black umbrellas had been deployed on its terrace and a group was actually sitting at one of them: a middle-aged couple with a grown-up daughter. A few tourists were buzzing about the mediæval honeycomb with Japanese cameras. In a niche below the memorial plaque to the *patriote* Vittorini, a small bunch of flowers, simple and moving, *anémones de Caen*, had been freshly placed today. Vittorini had not been hanged until July, 1944—a long time after Neville's visit, but Dr Aubin had said categorically that it was the result of that catastrophic mission. Would the village have been compulsorily turned out to witness the execution? What worthies would have been in the front rank, attesting in public their support for this version of law and order? It was unthinkable that Joseph Vittorini would not have measured up to the jaw-thrust of defiance demanded of him by convention.

Kenworthy went into the stationer's and bought the best map of the locality that they had in stock. Village shoppers gave courteous precedence to a visiting foreigner: perhaps they were only in there to gossip. Not many of them were old enough to have their roots in the same age as Joseph Vittorini and Chantal Dupuy: yet how many of them were talking this morning about the two Englishmen who had come to St Blaise? Kenworthy came back out into the Place de la Libération. An extraordinarily young policeman was dealing tactfully with a parking infringement before it could happen. The usual thoughts crossed Kenworthy's mind about the age of policemen. This one did not look a day older than eighteen. *Police Municipale*—probably the only officer in St Blaise, and closely controlled by the mayor, with local trivialities foremost among his duties. Kenworthy

went into the Café des Tilleuls, irrespective of the reception
he had had there last night. And if he was prepared to forget
it, so apparently were the staff and the habitués. Men made
slight changes in their stance, withdrew elbows to let him
through to the counter. There were a number of men from
North Africa—a great many Arabs were working on the
modish building sites up and down the old olive groves,
some of them probably immigrants of dubious legality. But
the Tilleuls also had a following of retired field labourers,
many of whom could speak personally of the times of
Chantal Dupuy, if only their tongues could be loosened—
and understood.

The man behind the bar was the same one who had given
Kenworthy short shrift the previous evening. He seemed
able to put his hostility behind him as if it had not happened.
He now treated Kenworthy as if they had enjoyed each
other's company over the bar for years. There was an elderly
gentleman at the end of the counter, better dressed than
most here and wearing a black beret—one did not seem to
see them so often these days. He had the narrow ribbon of
some state order in his lapel, a sparse and upright man,
whose military service had clearly been the most impressive
period of his life. He was adept at not letting Kenworthy
catch his eye.

And then there took place one of the daily phenomena of
St Blaise. From the church tower overlooking the Place
midday was announced by an unbeautiful bell. And within
three minutes Les Tilleuls was full. Shopkeepers, professional men, painters, plumbers and mechanics must have
been counting down the last lingering seconds of the fore-
noon. A shutter had rattled across the window of the
Pâtisserie with remarkable punctuality. Tarpaulins had
been stretched over pavement displays. The baker was in
Les Tilleuls now; so were the butcher and a group of young
men from the garage, all in the siren-suit uniform of their
parent petrol company. There was a strong smell of aniseed

in the air—*pastis* was the apéritif *de rigueur*. Kenworthy
also noticed that a girl had come in—it would have been
impossible not to have noticed her. The most ardent sup-
porter of Les Tilleuls could not have denied that the café
was grubby, its floor strewn with dog-ends and screwed-up
lottery tickets. Except for the tourists on the terrace and the
elderly gentleman at the end of the bar, everyone here was
in working clothes, the young mechanics oily, the Arabs
smeared with building-site clay. But the young lady was
different. She looked about twenty and stood not an inch
more than five feet. Her cosmetics were as immaculate as
a ceramic mask, which gave her a particularly doll-like
appearance. She had on a shortish purple summer frock
which accentuated a figure that she could surely have offered
for modelling.

She was wearing a solitaire diamond on her ring-finger
—she knew how to make sure that no one would miss it—
and appeared to be engaged to one of the garage-hands, for
she remained close to him on the fringe of the group,
not saying more than an occasional inaudible syllable, but
passing him the assurance of an adoring look from time to
time. She seemed to be the close friend of the entire team
from the garage—indeed of everyone in the bar. There
appeared to be something indefinably formal and *proper*
about her. Everyone seemed to have respect for her. But no
one except Kenworthy seemed in any way impressed by the
contrast between her appearance and the shabby décor.
Presumably they saw her like this every day at noon.

Kenworthy, ready for a second beer, was competing for
the barman's eye when a second phenomenon struck him.
He suddenly caught a whiff of Neville's smoking mixture.
Was it conceivable that the Colonel was somewhere among
this crowd? It was not impossible: he might have tucked
himself away in a corner. He had probably by now had all
the time to himself that he needed. Most likely he had been
over to Le Baou, had performed there his devotions or

whatever, had submitted to some sort of sentimental cathar-
sis and had come back to pick up such St Blaise acquain-
tances as were left. Not without difficulty, because the bar
was packed shoulder to shoulder. Kenworthy tried to see
into every cranny. He could see Neville nowhere. But then
he saw that the man in the corner, the one with the beret
and the decoration, had loaded a pipe. It was the only pipe
being smoked in here besides Kenworthy's own.

Kenworthy began to edge along the bar, to filter through
knots of cronies. A pipe-man was entitled to ask another
pipe-man what he was smoking. But before he could reach
him, the man emptied his glass—he was drinking an ordinary red wine—and put money down on the counter. Kenworthy too put money down and followed him out. He was
half way across the Place and moving at a nippy pace before
he caught up with him.

'Monsieur—'

With a frankly nervous look on his face, the man performed the reflex action of raising his hat.

'Monsieur—I'm sure you'll excuse me—'

Kenworthy tried to make a laughing matter of it, but the
man was not a laughing type.

'Your tobacco, Monsieur—the aroma of it. Could you tell
me where I could—?'

The man was itching to be on his way. It would have
been comic if it had not been so frustrating. He was torn
two ways. He did not wish to be discourteous, in the terms
of the codes of his youth. But he wanted to be off.

'Monsieur,' he said, 'I am sure your motives are admir-
able. But why do you come here?'

'Isn't St Blaise des Figuiers an interesting place to visit?'

This did not seem to impress the man. He was anxious
to the point of neurosis to make good his escape. It was as
if he did not even want to be seen in the street talking to
Kenworthy.

Kenworthy let him go. He saw that Les Tilleuls was

beginning to empty itself almost as rapidly as it had filled. *L'heure de l'apéritif* was yielding to the demands of family lunch-tables. The mechanics were leaving. The girl was putting on a crash-helmet, straddling her fiancé's pillion and being whisked noisily up a steep alley. The building workers went off, chattering in Arabic. Three old men parted in the street, each going towards a different house. Kenworthy caught up with the one who seemed to have the furthest to go.

'Excuse me—have you heard anything of another Englishman who spent last night in St Blaise?'

'Je n'en sais rien, monsieur.'

He too seemed scared of becoming involved with Kenworthy.

'Well, one more little thing,' Kenworthy said. 'Do you know the name of the gentleman—the one who was smoking the pipe?'

But the old man took the easiest way out and affected no longer to understand Kenworthy's French. He was already shuffling off.

And then the young policeman in the Place was waving down an oncoming lorry, clearing the way for a car that he had spotted coming up the dip from Fresnes. It was a pre-war Rolls—very considerably pre-war, with the square-cut lines that one associated with scratched, hazy news-reels of royal cortèges. The chauffeur was in a livery that exactly matched the bottle-green of the coachwork and there were two people in the back: a white-bearded old man with his head sunk between his shoulders and beyond him, masked by him so that Kenworthy could not see her properly, a younger but not young woman of imposing but not outsize proportions. The few people on the narrow pavements stood back as if to allow extra scope for their passage. The Rolls climbed towards the château on the rock summit of St Blaise.

Kenworthy spoke to the policeman: at least there seemed

something of the comfort of the cloth in questioning a
guardian of the peace.

'Who was that?'

The policeman looked as if anyone in St Blaise would
have advised him to answer none of this stranger's questions.
But he too was the puppet of two codes. After some seconds
he remembered that he was also supposed to be helpful to
tourists.

'That was Monsieur Jean-Paul Arribat, monsieur. He
used to be a judge in Marseilles.'

'And the lady who was with him?'

'I can't say, monsieur. I have not seen her before.'

If he knew by hearsay—which he certainly must—he was
not going to be the one to pass on the information to
Kenworthy.

'I wonder if you can tell me another thing. There was a
man in Les Tilleuls just now smoking a pipe.'

Again protracted consideration as to which loyalty should
win.

'I think you mean Monsieur Levaray, monsieur.'

'I must have a word with Monsieur Levaray. As a pipe-
smoker myself, I am intrigued by what he was smoking.'

'I know nothing at all about that, sir.'

And then the boyish-looking *agent* moved away, his
trained eye having spotted another car-movement that could
have caused a chain-reaction of jams. Parking was clearly
his most pressing problem. Kenworthy saw that the Rolls
had stopped thirty yards up the slope and that the passenger
had got out and was coming down towards him. She was
the sort of woman conveniently described as handsome:
meaning that what hindered her from actual beauty was
perhaps her conventional hairstyle, perhaps her expensive
but almost aggressively sober costume, more probably the
mental outlook that had enabled her to defeat the field in a
sub-world of exceptionally able men. Perhaps there was
something about her that was not quite as feminine as one

might wish for. Presumably this was Chantal Dupuy, the state prosecuting barrister who forty years ago had been selected from a cadre of women of last-ditch courage to do a task that one of the inscrutable masterminds behind the networks considered critical. When one heard of women in the Resistance movement, one thought of them in raincoats, on bicycles, evading road-blocks and snap checks on rural trains. Or else they were leading files of shot-down aircrew along mule-tracks over mountains. But fiction's picture was incomplete: fiction preferred the picturesque. Such women had also had to be able to recruit and hold together in the same traces communists and ultra-conservatives. They had needed to persuade sworn avengers that they were not doing the best they could for the community by casually murdering relatively innocent German soldiers on city pavements: that only brought down reprisals on hostages and entire communities. The likes of Chantal Dupuy had had to find ways of cornering rations in mind-boggling quantities. They had had to get them on the move to where they were sorely needed; and then to persuade the recipients to be satisfied with the inadequacy of what they got. They had had to be loyal to masters who had never met them, and whose imagination often stopped short of any real knowledge of what life was like beyond the murky Channel. They had had to inspire others with that confidence; to spread the gospel among weary, frightened, prejudiced people. When the prophet who dropped from the sky turned out as ill-starred as Neville had been, they had to steer him away from trouble and try to get him home again in one piece. How did it complicate matters if they also chanced to fall in love with him? Did that necessarily mean that they had been blind to his weaknesses?

Chantal Dupuy could have been twenty-four at the most when she had stood like Victor Hugo's Moses, powerful and solitary on the Sinai of Le Baou. By now solitary power would be no novelty to her. When she addressed herself to

Kenworthy, she did not seem in a mind to allow him much
latitude. Perhaps she was out of the habit of allowing latitude
to men.

'Are you the man who's with Rawdon Neville?'

Kenworthy tried to think of her as a woman who would
in her time have slept with or murdered any man—perhaps
the two consecutively—according to tactical exigency.
Nothing about her appearance fitted the image.

'I *was* with him.'

'What do you mean by that?'

Even before she phrased her first question, she seemed to
have decided that he was a hostile witness. On what possible
grounds?

'He gave me the slip,' Kenworthy said.

'Gave you the slip? Are you his keeper?'

It sounded as though one of her specialities was under-
mining the dignity of witnesses on principle.

'In a manner of speaking. We had come to terms with
that fact.'

'I do not know what that can possibly mean. Where is he
now?'

'I don't know. I'd been hoping that you'd be able to tell
me.'

She ignored that.

'When did you last see him?'

'The night before last.'

'Where?'

'Up in the forest.'

'I take it that you navigated more precisely than that?
Where, exactly? In which forest?'

'I can't be more precise. Neville had all the maps and
went off with them. They were his, after all. I can tell you
that it was near to a bridge that has collapsed.'

'What a peculiar route to take.'

'I thought that perhaps he was trying to retrace the way
by which he originally came.'

'Then he has forgotten the way he came—if he ever knew it.'

She looked at him with an expression that must have made many a prisoner at the bar believe that she personally hated him.

'Who are you, anyway?'

'Simon Kenworthy, Londoner, one time Detective Chief Superintendent, Metropolitan Police. I am occasionally— and almost always against my better judgement—persuaded to undertake private jobs for people.'

'Including the British Government?'

'Not this time. My brief is from Mrs Neville.'

Truth in its absolute simplicity was the only way he had of convincing her. But it would be fatal to be seen to be trying too hard to do that.

'I don't know the lady,' she said.

'Nor can I say that I do. I met her for long enough to accept the assignment.'

'Of which you seem to have made a mess.'

'I have temporarily lost the Colonel. It was always on the cards that I might. One man can't shadow another for twenty-four hours a day, even when their tents are side by side. I thought I'd traced him to Les Tilleuls by the smell of his pipe—but that turned out to belong to a Monsieur Levaray.'

'Charles Levaray. Have you talked to Charles?'

'He wouldn't talk back.'

'That doesn't surprise me. So what's your next move? Or should I not ask?'

'Le Baou. This afternoon, if I can organize transport.'

'I will organize transport. I will take you to Le Baou. I would like to see the Rock again. Have you lunched yet?'

'I haven't looked into the possibilities.'

'Come up to the château. But I should warn you, the Judge's midday table is frugal. And he is no Anglophile.'

CHAPTER 9

There was, Kenworthy supposed, something deeply characteristic of France about lunching with the Judge—characteristic at any rate of a seam of Frenchness to which the average Englishman rarely had the privilege of entry. And if it was true that Judge Arribat was an Anglophobe, this clearly took second place in his philosophy to his obligations as a host. He treated Kenworthy not only with dignity but with a sort of unspoken assurance that even friendship might be considered—after a few years' acquaintance.

There was a pricelessness behind the largely eighteenth-century setting that it was beyond Kenworthy's expertise to assess. But the life style in the château had about it a sort of high-level simplicity. The Judge had the Frenchman's mastery of the art of conversation, a structured interplay of wit and ideas. He served a *potage* from the tureen, followed by a platter of cold meats, a variety of regional cheeses and fresh fruit. The talk stayed strictly away from anything that had to do with Kenworthy's or Chantal Dupuy's reasons for being in St Blaise. And whether he hated all things English or not, he, like Mademoiselle, seemed better informed that the average man in the English street about what was going on in portentous corridors. It was as if they read *The Times* thoroughly at least twice a week. Both of them seemed to make frequent visits to London and the Judge discussed the English Disease without saying anything trite, artificial or barbed.

Not until Kenworthy was being offered a *fine* with his coffee did Mademoiselle show any awareness of the time. It was she who smoothly terminated the lunch-hour and got them away from St Blaise—in the Rolls, with the Judge's chauffeur at the wheel, but without the Judge.

Kenworthy was not clear at what stage Mademoiselle Dupuy had turned off her candid hostility, but he was under no illusion about the nature of her civility. It was no more than a tactical armistice. The terms of an eventual peace treaty had not been mooted. And she still did not say anything about Le Baou. The first surprise came as they were descending the steep hill south-westwards out of St Blaise. An open two-seater sports car was coming up, a souped-up 1930s model. A man in the blue uniform overalls of the St Blaise garage was driving and beside him sat the doll-like girl whom Kenworthy had had the chance to study in Les Tilleuls. Her hair was swept back by the breeze and she was screwing up her eyes against the onrush of air, but otherwise she preserved the appearance of a Dresden figurine sprung up in a musical box.

She smiled at Kenworthy as their cars passed, as if the fact of their having caught sight of each other in Les Tilleuls gave them a solid basis for friendship. This young lady was everybody's sweetheart—and expected to be. But Chantal Dupuy took no part in the interchange. She held her head stiffly, her eyes concentrating fixedly on the road ahead of them. She seemed anxious not to catch sight of the girl—not even accidentally.

Perhaps there was nothing in it. But Kenworthy could have quoted such strange moments from many a case—sensitive little incidents, vividly registered, and later to fill out with meaning.

The road twisted down towards a fertile plain—lavender, violets and roses were grown here under contract to the great perfumiers—and at one point they caught a glimpse of the Mediterranean, as blue in the distance as a pre-war advertisement for Reckitts. It was out in some such bay that Neville had started the last calamitous leg of his wartime trip.

The chauffeur picked up an obsolete voice-pipe and spoke to Mademoiselle Dupuy. She lifted her end of the instrument and, leaning forward to see exactly where they were, gave him brief instructions. He pulled in at the edge of the road, and Kenworthy saw that they were in for a climb that would have tested a younger man. Was Chantal Dupuy, like Neville, hoping to shame him with a display of unnatural physical fitness? He hoped not. She might be in better condition than the Colonel.

Access to the hillside was by a dirt road through a padlocked gate that the state prosecutor climbed without ceremony. The map that Kenworthy had bought this morning, despite its large scale, gave no indication of any lost village on this escarpment. Within very few minutes his companion was yards ahead of him. But when she came to a forking track, she stood, turned and waited for him, breathless and not sorry to pause. He came alongside her.

'To think,' she said, 'that I once drove two bullocks up here.'

It was the first reference she had made to 1943; the first indication she had given that war stories might be admissible conversation.

'Doing my best not to break the skyline more often than I could help.'

All part of the vast communal operation needed to protect the injured Neville?

But she showed impatience to continue the climb. Like Neville, she was trying to show off, although she was beginning to show signs of overheating—and finding that she, too, had put on a few years since she had last really exerted herself.

'We don't have to prove anything, you and I,' Kenworthy said. 'That was one of my troubles with our friend the Colonel. He had me in a constant state of physical inferiority. He seemed to need to have me on my knees—though he was sometimes hard put to it to conceal that he was on his knees himself.'

He hoped that they were now on the verge of reasonable

talk. But Chantal Dupuy remained a cautious woman.

'You're right. Let's take our time,' she said. 'Nobody's focusing telescopic sights on us today.'

Their footpath skirted an outcrop of denuded limestone. She scanned the hillside above them. Kenworthy knew that she was looking for something particular, and he could not see what it might be. They bore to the left, along a track of ruts and dust that showed no signs of having been trodden or ridden during the last few weeks—at least, not since it had last rained, whenever that was. On either side of them were the ubiquitous gnarled olive trees, an industry that had flagged in the face of competition from less conservative national economies. They passed the ruins of someone's hard-worked farm, a collapsed water-storage basin, an abandoned irrigation system.

It was easy to understand the sense of security of anyone hiding out in the ruins above them. They would have had an excellent command of any approach, would have seen any pinprick of light, would have had abundant notice of any petrol engine. The hill which bore Le Baou was only the beginning of a series of progressive elevations that folded into each other for miles away into the Alps and the Massif Central. With a guide who knew the safe ways across the interlocking valleys, a man on the run would have everything in his favour; provided, of course, he had not added a dislocated ankle to his and his comrades' hazards.

They climbed steadily for half an hour, then came across disconcerting evidence of recent human presence: a couple of small-bore cartridges lying at an intersection of what might just about deserve to be called footpaths.

'We were talking about the English Disease at lunch-time.'

Chantal Dupuy was disgusted.

'Here we have the French Disease—or one of them: *la chasse*. How can they have the nerve to call it hunting? In France, unlike your country, there's no social distinction about it. A man's simply not worth his salt if he doesn't own a sporting gun.'

'What are they after? Venison? Wild boar?'

She found that laughable.

'That's for those who can afford a stake in stocked and syndicated territory. Up here it's robins, thrushes, black-birds. Down on the plain it's larks: anything that stirs a feather is worth stalking.'

'These cartridges are fresh,' Kenworthy said. 'I'd say they'd been fired today. They have a mint look about them.'

'Oh yes—I dare say we shall hear shots—if there's any-thing alive left to shoot at.

As he looked uphill, foreshortened distances were decep-tive. Rough greenery stretched interminably ahead. Here and there they found litter—litter of any kind always fasci-nated Kenworthy. He was always grasping for something of the personalities that had passed. But nothing that they found on the way up to Le Baou taught him anything: a squashed plastic container that had held supermarket bleach; an empty Stella Artois can. Who the hell came up here carrying bleach?

Onwards and upwards. They found a fresh dog-turd. The robin-hunter's companion? Then they saw a heavily weathered notice-board, nailed to a tree: *La Chasse* in these woods was strictly preserved for a club domiciled in Fresnes les Puits. They climbed for another thirty-five minutes be-fore coming upon the first evidence of Le Baou—but it was little more than another scattering of litter. Last year's picnics? Some petty criminal on the run and sleeping rough? Ever since he had first heard of the place, Kenworthy had wondered why there was no mention in the guide-books of the medieval vestiges of a community whose posterity still existed, probably with many of the same surnames, on another rock not more than four miles away as one drew a straight line. But now he could see: any guide-book that encouraged hopeful sightseers to undertake this climb was

going to lose its credibility. There was hardly anything more
than a change in the pattern of vegetation to make anyone
look twice. There were indeed a few lumps of stone, like the
stumps of molars in a pauper's mouth. They might have
been the lower edges of house-walls: no—not *might*—*must*
have been. Someone had lived in the homes that had stood
here: here the village cobbler, here the village drunk, there
the village lady-killer. And where was there any relic of the
wartime occupation? Where had men actually *lived*? Where
had they even taken shelter? Nowhere could he see any
dugout or cavern, any roof to cover a man's head.

'Mademoiselle—where did the Maquis live when they
were in possession?'

'There were cellars under some of the rubble. You know
how they built in the Middle Ages. There were houses under
houses.'

'But I see no trace of that now. What has happened to
the place?'

'I don't know,' she said in a burst of impatience that
sounded very like the effect of cumulative suppressed ten-
sion. 'And don't expect me to know. I never belonged to
this region. I was brought here to do a specific task. I was
told no more than what they thought I ought to know—
and that was not always as much as I needed to know.'

'It's a wonder that the system worked.'

'On Le Baou it didn't. Surely you've gathered at least
that for yourself by now.'

She wandered some yards away from him and he could
tell that there was some particular spot that she was trying
to look for—and that she did not want him to share what
she had in mind. She wanted to get ahead of him to look at
things for herself, and whenever he reached her side, she
moved away again impatiently. He followed her up to a
former terrace, almost completely hidden under a tangle of
flowering weeds. Here it was marginally more apparent that
this had once been a human habitat. The grasses had been

more recently trodden. Chantal Dupuy followed a furrow
made by feet through weeds, stood looking down into a
hollow that might at some time have been the foundations
of a dwelling. She beckoned to Kenworthy.

'Do you recognize that?'

Almost completely concealed under vegetation, he saw
the slashed and shredded remains of a bright blue rucksack,
torn away from its tubular frame. The frame itself was not
to be found.

'Colonel Neville's.'

'You're sure of that?'

'I ought to know. I looked at it for days on end: it was
usually in front of me. You think this is to do with something that happened forty years ago? It looks like ordinary
vandalism to me—as if he simply ran into ruffians.'

'No,' she said.

'Well, that's a firm answer, even if it's a bald one.'

'He didn't run into ruffians.'

'You seem certain.'

'I am certain. I've seen all this before.'

But before she could go into detail, they heard a shot,
somewhere on the perimeter of the ruins: a single barrel. To
mark a sparrow's fall? They stood stock still. The echo took
a long time to die. A bird flew frantically out of a tree, as if
it were the last wild creature left on the hillside.

Before they could move away, a man came towards them
from out of the trees—a man with a gun under his arm, its
breech open. He was one of the Arab building-workers
whom Kenworthy had seen in Les Tilleuls before lunch.

'Who are you?' Chantal Dupuy asked him. 'Have you a
permit to be carrying that thing? Come to that, I'm tempted
to wonder if you have a labour permit, either.'

He had the look about him of a simple man who liked
to make friends with people. He was crestfallen at her
aggression.

'How long have you been up here?'

'An hour.'

'Have you seen anyone else?'

'Not until you came.'

'Have you a dog with you?' Kenworthy asked him, remembering the dropping they had seen lower down.

'No. No dog.'

'And you've not seen anyone with a dog?'

'No man. No dog.'

'Let me look at your gun.'

Kenworthy examined it briefly.

'The cartridges we saw just now were a different bore from this. There's been someone else on the hill. He's probably still here.'

She leaped forward without warning and seized the Arab by a lapel.

'I could make trouble for you. You know that. Whose gun is this? Your own?'

'I borrowed it from a friend.'

'Which could make trouble for your friend too. He'll not thank you if you get his gun confiscated. We're going to ask you some questions. Some of them we've asked you already. If you want to change any of your answers, this will be your last chance. But if you tell us any lies, we shall take you straight to the Gendarmerie. Understood?'

'It is understood, madame.'

He was trying very hard to establish the impression of a friendly, honest, naïve man.

'You've seen nobody but us on Le Baou? No man with a dog?'

'Nobody at all. But I will show you something.'

Kenworthy caught sight of a lizard basking in sunshine on a stone—delicate, motionless. Lizards were a comparative rarity in Kenworthy's life—but this was no time to be paying attention to them.

The North African turned and began walking back in the direction from which he had come, looking back over his

shoulder to make sure that they were following. They crossed
the upper perimeter of the lost village, slithered down a
bank and reached another footpath of a kind, a hunter's
footpath. They were approaching the slope of the valley that
separated them from the next great hill. This path could
have been one of the *maquisards'* escape routes when Le Baou
was threatened.

The Arab stopped and stooped towards the roots of what
Kenworthy was later to identify as a castor-oil tree. It looked
at first as if what the Arab was showing them was a
body—then it looked like something covering a body.
Then Kenworthy saw that it was a sleeping-bag—Neville's
sleeping-bag, recognizable from the maker's name-tag.
And it had been savagely and repeatedly slashed. Kenworthy picked it up, carried it over to an open space and
inspected it. It had been out in at least one night's dews
and insects were already taking advantage of its folds.

'No blood,' Kenworthy said. 'He wasn't in it when it was
slashed.'

'Even if there'd been blood, it wouldn't have worried me.
He left blood behind on a tattered shirt once. But he hadn't
been hurt.'

'Is this a story that you're going to tell me?'

Middle-aged, angry with herself at discovering that she
was not in the trim that she would have liked to be, it
seemed more difficult than ever to picture her in her vigorous
early twenties.

'He was blazing a trail—but not in order to tell people
where he'd gone. He was trying to send them the wrong
way. I think I can claim to know your Colonel better than
you do—some things about him, anyway. He did this once
when he was here. He liked to show the makings of a clever
man—but he was seldom clever enough. He laid a trail
over several miles, littering belongings conspicuously behind
him: a shirt here, a bloodstained handkerchief there, the
wrapping from a tobacco packet. Then he doubled back on

himself. And all because he believed Le Baou was about to be attacked—he didn't wait to ask those of us who knew something about it. He even thought he was *au fait* with the local topography—after a matter of days, for most of which he had been immobilized. Whenever Colonel Neville did any thinking for himself, he was a menace. He said he wanted to avoid casting suspicion on any helpers he might find along the route he intended to take. What he didn't realize was how much suspicion he was casting on innocents along his false trail. Two good men were taken into investigative custody. You know what that meant. And for no other reason than that they farmed along the track that Colonel Neville pretended to have taken. You'll see their name up in the village: Vittorini.'

'Shouldn't we be careful about jumping to conclusions? For an open-air man as dedicated as Neville to jettison both his pack and his sleeping bag—'

'He can replace them both within twenty-four hours. This place might look lonely, but he'll never be more than three hours from a street with shops, and people who'd run messages for him. No, Mr Kenworthy. This seems to me typical of Colonel Neville—sentiment, living it all again.'

'You've a fair notion, I suppose, of where he actually will have gone?'

'I have an idea. Only an idea.'

'Aren't you going to tell me?'

'It would mean nothing to you. On your own you would never find it.'

'I'll be guided by you entirely, mademoiselle. Should we or should we not follow him?'

'Not now, certainly. It's a good four hours' rough slog from here on foot, and it would be dark long before we got back.'

'Surely there's a nearer approach from a by-road somewhere?'

'There is—but I wouldn't care to entrust the Judge's Rolls to it.'

'Don't think I'm doubting you,' Kenworthy said. 'But it seems to me that we shouldn't take too much for granted.'

'I tell you, I know how Rawdon Neville's mind works. I had plenty of opportunities to sample his intelligence—too many of them. There are moments when you might even think he had a brain—but you never got far without crashing into its limits.'

'You don't think we should cover ourselves by reporting what we've found?'

'Not unless you want to find yourself bogged down with long-winded and incompetent officials, answering questions and signing affidavits at the pace set by French bureaucracy. And you'd be unable ever after to move a kilometre without being watched.'

'You should be in a position to know about that.'

'I do. And I'm sure you don't want to lose your independence of action. What matters more to me, I don't want to lose mine.'

So they returned through the stronghold vestiges of Le Baou, went down at a leisurely pace to where the Rolls was parked, and drove back up to St Blaise, where Mademoiselle dropped Kenworthy at his own request at the bottom of the Rue du Château.

He found himself an obscure corner by a window of Les Tilleuls from which he could keep the entire Place under observation. He had been there about an hour when he saw the bonnet of the Rolls sliding almost silently down again. The chauffeur in livery was not now at the wheel—Chantal Dupuy was. And at her side sat Dr Aubin.

They drove off in the direction in which Mademoiselle Dupuy had taken Kenworthy to Le Baou. And scarcely had they left the village before Kenworthy saw another figure that he knew cross his front. Monsieur Charles Levaray

came down from the direction in which he had gone to his
home before lunch: a fragile-looking, fleshless figure with
the gait of an old man—only this time he had a companion:
Dr Aubin's Madame Ripault. For a moment it looked as if
they were about to cross and come into Les Tilleuls. But
then they went on, over the forecourt of the garage and in
through its office door. They were in there for several
minutes and then there was some shunting about of standing
cars to allow a large black Citroën to be brought out. It
was being driven by the blue-overalled mechanic whom
Kenworthy had seen earlier on in the red sports car. His
mask-faced fiancée was sitting with him in the front.
Monsieur Levaray and Madame Ripault got into the back.
Did the girl go with her boyfriend on all his hired journeys?
They too drove off along the road that could take them to
Le Baou—or beyond.

CHAPTER 10

Kenworthy stayed at his table in Les Tilleuls until early
evening. He had an unsatisfying paperback in his pocket,
turned its pages at intervals, looking up, sharpening his ears
whenever someone strange to him came in. But he neither
heard nor saw anything that appeared to have any bearing
on main events. He saw none of the principals return to St
Blaise—but once daylight began to fail, he was no longer
able to identify the occasional vehicle that entered the
village. He heard a car turn into the garage, but could not
see who got out of it.

The old man with the watery eyes, who yesterday evening
had eaten fried eggs, came in and was served with a bowl
of brawn. He did not ask for a menu, did not choose what
they brought him. It looked as if Les Tilleuls was under
contract to serve him a cheap evening meal. Kenworthy too

asked for food, and today was courteously and more than amply served.

He was beginning to realize how tired he was and the thought of the walk back to Fresnes les Puits horrified him. He went over to the garage to see if there was any active life—and within ten minutes was being driven to his hotel by the affianced mechanic, who asked permission to bring his striking girlfriend with them. She still had the china doll look of earlier in the day. What was it about her that had affected Chantal Dupuy? She was far too young to be Mademoiselle's daugher. Her grand-daughter, perhaps? And in that case Neville's grand-daughter? It was remarkable how many cases in Kenworthy's book had turned on unmanageable domestic situations.

The drive to Fresnes took no more than five minutes, during which time the lovers did not speak to each other. The boyfriend was a clean-shaven, clear-eyed youth. It was difficult to know whether he was yet mature enough to have developed real character. Together they looked decent enough, naïve without being simple: a characteristic couple about to embark on the ups and downs of late-twentieth-century marriage.

At the *auberge* Kenworthy's landlady gave the impression that she had been watching for his arrival. She looked precisely as she had looked at breakfast-time: her hair in the intricate black pile that was all but ludicrous.

'Monsieur Kenworthy, I've found someone who'll be able to tell you all you want to know.'

'That's the sort of situation I like to find myself in,' Kenworthy said, but when he saw who it was, the issue seemed more clouded than ever.

Madame Piquemal had arranged the meeting for nine o'clock and took an intriguer's pleasure in keeping dark the identity of the man who was coming. Was it a national trait to love mystery for its own sake—or were the habits of mind of forty years ago still dying hard?

Kenworthy went upstairs and continued the letter home that he had started in Nice. Madame rang him on the house-phone when his informant arrived. As Kenworthy came down again to meet him, he caught the unmistakable whiff of herbal smoking mixture. Madame Piquemal had put the austere, inscrutable—and up to now frigidly un-friendly—Monsieur Levaray into an annexe of the breakfast-room and given him an apéritif. Even now, Monsieur Platon, as she called him, did not seem to begin to share her enthusiasm for the coming interview. He greeted Kenworthy with stiff and monosyllabic formality. He had a deep and pleasant voice, and although Kenworthy was no academic linguist, he had no difficulty in recognizing that this was French of a pedantic, classical polish—far removed from the speech ordinarily heard at zinc-topped counters. At least Levaray was mercifully easier to understand.

'Monsieur Platon was Commandant of Le Baou,' Madame Piquemal said from the corner of her mouth as she left them to it.

Kenworthy offered M. Platon a second Cinzano, which he declined. He set himself up with a beer. *Platon*—Plato: many wartime operators had chosen classical pseudonyms. Célimène—Dorante—Agrippine had all been the *noms de guerre* of operators.

'So—I believe you can tell me something about the *Résistance* in St Blaise?'

'There are others who could tell you more.'

'But I believe—'

What did he believe?

'*Madame la patronne* assures me—'

'In so far as *la Résistance* in St Blaise amounted to anything at all, I will answer your questions to the best of my ability.'

Stiffly—as if he resented being put in this position.

'You say it did not amount to very much. But your Le Baou was a centre, wasn't it, for effective *maquisards*?'

'There were *maquisards* on Le Baou. It is debatable how

effective they were. And Le Baou was hardly an operations centre.'

'I see. Or, at least, I don't see. But I suppose that gives us a *point de départ.*'

Kenworthy looked at him with exaggerated brightness, waiting for him to start talking. But the man looked more withdrawn than ever. Kenworthy brought out his pipe and pouch and offered Plato a fill.

'Or do you smoke nothing but your herbs?'

'I gave them up as soon as we could get decent tobacco again. Yes—I would be glad to try what you are smoking.'

Kenworthy waited till they both had cores of tobacco smouldering.

'The herbs were double-pronged,' Plato said laconically. 'Tobacco worth smoking was hard to come by, and our mixture served as a password.'

'And you needed a password for Colonel Neville's return? Were you afraid you would not recognize each other?'

'We can hardly expect to look like the men we used to be, Monsieur Kenworthy—'

It really did sound as if the man had no sense of humour.

'But mostly it was, shall I say, a sentimental gesture.'

So he was capable of that.

Which did at least establish that Plato and Neville had got together: not exactly a surprise—but this was the first concrete admission that Kenworthy had had that any of Neville's wartime contacts had met him again.

'Tell me something more about the role that Le Baou played in your movement,' Kenworthy asked.

Plato struggled. For some reason—it must surely be an obscure one—he did not like the question.

'Le Baou played a very minor part.'

Plato stopped talking—either because talking itself was an occupation that he found unsympathetic, or because he was by inner nature reluctant to risk giving anything away.

Then he seemed to come to a decision and started talking again, as if it were an unpalatable duty.

'Le Baou was not a nerve-centre. It played little part in cosmic operations. It was a position that we kept very lightly manned, so that the Gestapo and the Maréchal's Milice would believe that it was worth wasting manpower on. They kept watch on it. They even believed that it was occasionally worth raiding. It pinned some of their patrols down, and enabled us to get on with more vital activities elsewhere.'

Plato struck a match.

'One man alone on that hillside could create the desired impression. He made a little noise now and then, showed a seemingly careless light. In the evening he would sometimes show a plume of supper-fire smoke. If the Boche decided to come up and investigate, he had plenty of time to make himself scarce.'

'And the real *maquisards*—the ones who mattered?'

Plato was evidently uncertain whether he ought to answer this, even at this range of time.

'St Blaise was not an operational command of great importance. It was a rallying point for men—and some women—who were fleeing from other commands that had been attacked, betrayed or compromised. But it was only a report and dispersal centre. When people arrived here, we moved them on as quickly as we could.'

'And how far from Le Baou was your active head-quarters?'

'Not more than a ravine or two away—but it was a tricky stretch to cover, even for a man who knew where he was going.'

For a moment he sounded as if he might be beginning to warm to story-telling.

'Every last ounce of our stores had to be dragged uphill and down-valley on sleds. Dragged up Le Baou, too. We also had to keep stores there—some—enough to keep up appearances. We had rifles for which we had no ammunition, and bullets of the wrong calibre: enough to make a raiding party believe that it really was an HQ.'

'And how often was Le Baou raided?'

'Several times. This, by the way, Monsieur Kenworthy, is the most excellent tobacco I have ever smoked.'

'I have a small reserve upstairs. Remind me to give you a couple of packets before you go.'

'That's very kind of you. But I don't think you are going to find out much that will interest you in St Blaise, Monsieur Kenworthy.'

'But you and your friends a few ravines away—you are not going to tell me that they were inactive?'

'You call them my friends. I had no friends on Le Baou, Monsieur Kenworthy. The war threw contrasting companions together.'

'But didn't contrasting companions often become staunch comrades?'

'Sometimes they didn't. Sometimes they disagreed even over minor tactics. We were all fighting the same enemy— but not all for the same cause.'

'And when orders came from London, you were not always equally happy about them?'

'When orders came from London, it as often as not meant trouble for St Blaise.'

There was a new fluency in his speech now.

'I'm not questioning that we were allies. We had a lot of left-wingers, some of them excellent fighting men. But they were not risking their lives in order to consolidate Western capitalism. Some of them were out and out bolsheviks. Others among us were as right-wing as anything France has ever produced. Our common cause was France. We did our best to remember that—but we did not always all agree what France meant. Sometimes we needed to be reminded. By the likes of Chantal Dupuy. That was one of the jobs that she came here to do—and she was astringent. She always did have the makings of a disciplinarian.'

Plato had packed his pipe too tightly with Kenworthy's unfamiliar flake, and was frequently having to relight it.

'I will tell you a story. When Chantal Dupuy first came here, she was not the orthodox figure she's known as nowadays. She had the reputation of a red-ragging leftist, the protagonist of everything that was anathema to the old school. There was an elderly woman of property living in the hills—long since deceased—Madame Henriette Cazargue. She hadn't heard the name de Gaulle till she picked it up listening illegally to the BBC—and from then on she was Gaulliste to the marrow. She was a faithful churchwoman who in her time would have been an ultramontane—conservative triple distilled. Mademoiselle Dupuy had called on her to try to negotiate eggs and vegetables for extra mouths we had to feed. The two women hated what each other stood for just about as much as two women could. But Madam Cazargue made a little speech.

'"You and I are oceans apart, mademoiselle—but you are young enough to get about and do things that I no longer can. So I place myself under your orders until we are liberated."

'But that was not the way it always worked out. Especially among the lesser men the interim sometimes loomed larger than the objective. There were some who wanted to kill for the sake of killing. There were some who would sacrifice women and children to blow up a country mansion because it housed a handful of Boche General Staff. Sometimes orders were disobeyed. When Chantal Dupuy came here, there were some who believed that she would be unable to get her orders obeyed. She taught some men a severe lesson.'

'Mademoiselle Dupuy could be harsh?'

'We were at war, Monsieur Kenworthy.'

'She was fundamentally a feminist?'

'Through and through.'

Not, Kenworthy imagined, that Levaray approved of feminism.

'She was in no way in command here?'

'No. She came on a special assignment to serve as Colonel Neville's executive officer—to make possible the job he was sent here to do. And to see that he had all the protection that was possible.'

Kenworthy knew he had to plunge.

'Were Colonel Neville and Chantal Dupuy in love with each other?'

Levaray looked aghast at the question. There was a narrowness in his character that made it impossible for him to answer it. For a moment Kenworthy decided to thrust on.

'So you are not going to tell me whether the Colonel was the father of Chantal Dupuy's child?'

'That is something that you cannot possibly expect me to discuss.'

Kenworthy had to abandon the tack.

'I have gathered—in fact Colonel Neville has told me himself—that his purpose in coming here was to hold discussions with a German.'

'That is so.'

'That must have caused mixed reactions in the men under your command. There must have been some who had little taste for direct negotiations with a Boche.'

'It was our rôle to carry out the orders that came to us.'

Inflexible: the man was giving unwitting testimony about what sort of leader he had been. But Kenworthy was giving up hope of learning what he wanted to learn.

'And what impression did you form of Colonel Neville?'

'I think one of the bravest men I ever met; one of the most straightforward—and the most reliable.'

'What can you tell me about the German?'

'He was an intelligent youngster with a half-finished degree in philosophy, and he came from a good family in the Palatinate. His father, being a Freemason, had been in bad odour with the Brownshirts since their earliest days. I think perhaps it was the Masonic connection that had him listened to in London. He was a deserter from the Occupation *Wehrmacht*. He had lived—or, rather, had almost failed to live—for a few weeks on his wits up in the Franche-Comté. Here he eventually got in touch with a local Resistance group—a very dangerous business from everybody's point of view: he was lucky not to be shot without question when he made his first approach. As it chanced, he managed to get them to listen to him. He said there was a group of young German soldiers in the same position as himself. If they were given support and a command framework, they would make themselves useful to the Allies in any number of ways, in view of the invasion that was obviously coming: sabotage, information, troop movements, news of fortifications and demolitions. It was all dutifully reported to London on the usual radio nets. Obviously it came to the ears of someone who took it seriously.'

'It appears to have proved a costly exercise for St Blaise, Monsieur Platon.'

'We considered ourselves on active service. Active service was frequently a costly business.'

'And do you think that from the point of view of results, this exercise was worth the cost?'

'We were never told the outcome of the exercise,' Levaray said, with the stiffness of a man who accepted that as a normal and proper decision of the military hierarchy.

Levaray was a man apparently without spark of any kind. He was an old man, older than his years, resigning himself to a dignified slow-down in his early sixties. Perhaps even in youth he had opted for dullness and conformity. It was difficult to think that he could have achieved much as Commandant of Le Baou—except to alienate those more fiery spirits who wanted to see things moving. Including Chantal Dupuy?

Levaray had obviously not wanted to prolong the inter-

view, for he had ordered the car from St Blaise for half past
nine. Kenworthy was relieved to see him go. He heard them
dip down into the intervening valley and climb back out of
it. He pictured the doll-like girl, without doubt still smiling
in the front passenger seat.

CHAPTER 11

Kenworthy slept badly, his common reaction when a case
was at a blind stage—when there was either too much or
too little evidence, and nothing looked as if it would ever
make sense. In a couple of decades from now there would
be nobody left who had had a footing in St Blaise in 1943.
Clearly it was Neville's return that had brought Chantal
Dupuy here. Could anyone but a Frenchman hope to get to
the bottom of it?

No answers. Then came tentative answers. Then there
spiralled a tangle of tentative answers that he had already
rejected. It was not a brain-storm, it was a brain-blizzard,
ideas savagely whipping and drifting this way and that.
He fell asleep so late that he woke late—or, rather, was
awakened by the pompously coiffured Madame Piquemal
calling him on the house-phone.

'You have visitors, Monsieur Kenworthy.'

'Who?'

'I think you had better come down,' she said.

Cloaks and daggers again. She had rung off before he
could press her for an answer.

He shaved and dressed quickly. Two men were waiting
for him down in the breakfast-room—one of them reading
the landlady's newspaper, the other writing with close concentration in a notebook. They both looked up as he came
in. The one with the notebook snapped it shut and put it
away in an inside pocket. He would be about forty, with

dark, lady-killing looks. His companion was younger—very young—and had the physique of a bruiser, with his head shaved almost to the scalp. His mouth had a droop about it that could easily become surly: the sort of man who might rapidly become bored by a peaceful existence.

Madame was hovering.

'Shall I serve your breakfast, sir?'

Kenworthy looked at his callers.

'Would you gentlemen care for a bowl of coffee?'

'No, thank you. And if you wouldn't mind putting your breakfast off for half an hour, sir—'

Polite—but they neither expected nor intended him to demur. Police: the hallmarks were international—solidity, stolidity, a heavy-moving carefulness. These were probably highly intelligent men, but they gave the appearance of wits blunted by rigidity of procedure. Yet Kenworthy knew that even this could be a delusion within a delusion.

The senior man produced his identity. Fayard. *Inspecteur.* PJ. Not just Police—*Police Judiciaire—crème de la crème.*

'Your name is Kenworthy? An Englishman? You came here the day before yesterday from Nice?'

'Not directly from Nice. A friend and I have been on a walking-tour.'

'A friend?'

'Yes. It's a longish story. I'll be quite happy to start at the beginning.'

Though he was by no means certain at this stage how much of it he was going to tell.

'Perhaps you know that I am a retired Chief Superintendent from Scotland Yard.'

If they had not smelled his cloth yet, it was better to let them know about it from the outset. Watching their reactions closely, he decided that they did not know already. Nor were they impressed.

'To save time, may we go straight on to how you spent yesterday?' Fayard asked him.

'Of course.'

And Kenworthy smiled.

'I shall have to go back into the past a bit if you are to make sense of any of it. What is this about?'

'It's about how you spent yesterday, monsieur.'

'Well, I spent the night here. I breakfasted here. Then I spent the inside of the morning talking to Dr Aubin in St Blaise.'

No need at this juncture to say anything about his journey in the back of the van. But his attempt to suppress it did not last seconds.

'Then—'

'Just one moment. How did you travel from here to St Blaise?'

'In the back of a medical supply van.'

'What an extraordinary way to make the journey! Why?'

'The lift had been arranged for me by Dr Aubin's house-keeper.'

If they did not know the lady, it was going to be difficult to give a credible account of her. The thought occurred to him that if they had had a first-hand account from someone who had seen him arrive in that van, they might have formed undesirable notions about his motives—or his sanity.

'Why did you go to see Dr Aubin?'

'I had lost the friend with whom I had been walking. He is a sick man, he needs drugs. I thought he might have been to see the doctor professionally.'

'You say you'd lost your friend. Have you found him yet?'

'No.'

'When did you last see him, and where?'

'Up in the forest. I don't know the name of the place— or even whether it has a name. Again, it was the day before yesterday. I had better explain to you how we came to be travelling together.'

But Fayard was determined that he should tell it in his way, not in his own. Kenworthy recognized the routine. It was intended to establish and maintain the dominance of the interviewer. It put a formality into the dialogue that he would have preferred to be without. But there was no point in trying not to go along with it. If he antagonized them, they were entitled to assume he had something sinister to hide.

'And after you left Dr Aubin?'

'I went to Les Tilleuls.'

'Did you speak to anyone there?'

'No. But I spoke to one or two people after I came out.'

'What people?'

'Three old men. An old gentleman called Charles Levaray. Then a very young member of the *Police Municipale* of St Blaise. Then Mademoiselle Dupuy.'

'Mademoiselle Dupuy?'

Kenworthy smiled at the Inspector again—though he was well aware by now that he was the only one doing any smiling.

'Chantal Dupuy—I thought she was a national figure.'

'What I mean, Monsieur Kenworthy, is why especially did you want to talk to her?'

'I wanted to know whether she had any news of my friend.'

'Why should she have?'

'They had worked together on a wartime operation, and I think that this is the reason why both of them have come here now.'

'And where did you go with her?'

'She took me to lunch with her host, a retired Judge, Monsieur Arribat, up at the château.'

'Then?'

'Then we went together to Le Baou.'

'Le Baou?'

The Inspector was playing it in a way that Kenworthy found wearisome. By pretending to know nothing at all, he was trying to compel Kenworthy to go into naïve detail, hoping to trip him into unwittingly saying more than he meant to. Kenworthy gave him a thumbnail sketch of Le Baou and briefly described his own impressions of the place.

'What did you do at Le Baou?'

'We looked around. We spoke to an Arab who was shooting sparrows.'

'Can you describe him?'

Kenworthy did his best, though he did not find it easy to differentiate between Arabs. His description was not one of which, as a former professional person, he felt proud. He also mentioned the finding of the rucksack and Neville's slashed sleeping-bag.

'So you must have thought that your friend had met with a very bad misadventure—probably a fatal one? Did you make any report to the authorities? To anyone?'

'No.'

'Isn't that an odd way to have behaved?'

Up to now neither policeman had been taking notes—just listening closely, the younger one with an incipient lip-curl of cynical disbelief. Now Fayard brought out a rather splendid silver ballpoint, a gift-set model that he began to play with. But he still did not produce his notebook.

'Well—don't you think it's odd? You are concerned because you have lost a friend—a sick friend. You go to considerable lengths to try to find him. You set about finding him by methods some of which, you must surely admit, are strange in the extreme. Then when you find traces of him —traces that are highly suggestive of foul play—you do nothing about it. For the next few hours you sit at a café table reading a paperback novel until it is nearly dark.'

So however little groundwork Fayard had done so far, he had taken the trouble to check on Kenworthy's afternoon movements in St Blaise. That would not have taken him long. People would have been eager to talk about the idiosyncrasies of a foreigner—and a friend of *notre petit voisin* at that.

'I think we need a few footnotes to your behaviour, monsieur.'

Well, Kenworthy could provide them. Every decision he had made had seemed reasonable at the time.

'Mademoiselle Dupuy knows more about Colonel Neville than I do. She knew him at a time of stress and quick-witted escapes. The rucksack and the damaged sleeping-bag were similar to a decoy trail he had laid in the neighbourhood of Le Baou during the war to send his pursuers in the wrong direction. She thought he was playing at repeating history.'

'And who were Colonel Neville's pursuers yesterday?'

'I don't know. There may not have been anybody. He might have been afraid that someone like Mademoiselle Dupuy or myself would come disturbing his privacy. You must understand, Monsieur, that Colonel Neville was on a pilgrimage. He was reliving his past. Perhaps this sounds sentimental, but I think he was a sentimental man. He was visiting certain places and people. He thought it might be the last time he would see them.'

'What people?'

'I can't tell you. The Colonel was very close about certain episodes in his past. Mademoiselle Dupuy might have been one of them.'

'But you said just now that he might have been avoiding Mademoiselle Dupuy. You are suggesting that he had enemies in this neighbourhood?'

'I am not in a position to know that. It's not improbable. The roots of all this go back to a time of mistrust. But you should bear in mind that the Colonel is seventy-five if he's a day. His local enemies, if he has any, are likely to be in the same age-bracket.'

But for how many generations might dormant malice remain lethal?

'I am sure, *Monsieur l'Inspecteur*, you would find it rewarding to talk to Mademoiselle Dupuy about her former associate.'

It would be a confrontation that Kenworthy would enjoy watching, if Chantal Dupuy took it into her head to tie the PJ in a few discomforting knots.

'You know so much about these affairs, Monsieur Kenworthy, yet you keep claiming to know so little.'

'That is because you will not allow me to talk about events in their logical sequence.'

So Kenworthy won that day, and the Inspector's sense of humour was not strong enough for him to see the funny side of it: the former pro having his own way with today's man.

Now the muscular young sergeant started taking everything down. Kenworthy omitted nothing that was vital. But he produced no major responses and only brief working questions when some ambiguity—or one of his less idiomatic French phrases—needed confirmation.

'So, Monsieur Fayard, there you have it. I hope I need not say that I am totally at your service. I am anxious to do anything I can to be helpful. And now—'

Fayard did not look as if he appreciated any offer of help outside his established drills.

'I shall want a written statement of all you have just told me. If you will come—'

'I am perfectly capable of making a plain deposition without the need for prompting,' Kenworthy said. 'It's the only kind of statement I would consider making. I certainly do not propose to take down a statement from anyone's dictation, and it would be a waste of an officer's time, employing him to watch me write. I promise I will start on it, immediately you have allowed me to breakfast.'

'*Pardon, Monsieur*—please do not let me keep you any longer from your *café au lait*. I must also warn you that the *juge d'instruction* will be wanting to talk to you.'

The examining magistrate—the French way of doing things—the lawyer who directed in detail the case-work of the detective, who interviewed witnesses, psychiatrists, social investigators—and the defendant; who decided what, if anything, was to be put before the court.

It was inevitable. And as Chantal Dupuy had forecast yesterday, French bureaucracy could be liberally wasteful of other people's time.

'And now, perhaps, you will lift a corner of the veil for me?'

It had been professionally efficient of Fayard not to reveal what crime had been committed. Kenworthy had not pressed to know, because he knew he would be wasting his time. In reversed circumstances he would have conducted the interview in the same way himself, sitting tight on what he knew, hoping that his man would say something to condemn himself. But now that he had come through the process without condemning himself, surely—

'I must ask you not to leave the neighbourhood without letting us know your intentions.'

The Inspector produced his printed card, to which he added a local telephone number and extension.

'Am I then under some sort of open arrest?'

'Not at all. You have said you wish to be helpful, and I am taking you at your word. Of course, that presupposes doing nothing that might be unhelpful.'

He was obviously going to consult with his *juge d'instruction* with the least possible delay.

The *juge d'instruction*: there were going to be exasperating inroads into Kenworthy's leisure and freedom of movement. He ate two *croissants*, asked Madame for paper, and began composing his statement. If Rawdon Neville had been found lying dead in some side-valley, it was going to be tricky explaining why he had not brought in the *gendarmerie* to look at the rucksack and sleeping-bag. It was beginning to be tricky explaining that, even to himself.

He did not as yet even know what was being investigated. He did not know whether he was a suspect or not. If things became difficult, he might need someone to do some devilling for him. Chantal Dupuy? No: she was directly

involved. It was even likely she was pursuing some devious-
ness on her own account. It would pay him not to dabble
with anyone on the inside of the case.

He went to the phone-booth and dialled a Nice number,
l'Agence St Hubert; Monique Colin—the ravishing little
mélange of sun-tan and leg-warmers who had saved his
bacon at the Aéroport. She had said she was mobile and
eager to be of assistance. And Agnes Neville would pick up
the bill.

CHAPTER 12

Rumour spread through Fresnes les Puits like sparks along
a trail of spilled gunpowder. Since he had no business there,
Kenworthy judged it discreet to stay away from St Blaise
today. But the word had lost no time in descending one
steep fortified hill and climbing its neighbour. The cafés of
Fresnes were alive with it: the body of Chantal Dupuy had
been found in a ditch at a farm-track crossroads up at Les
Carreaux, old Besson's place on the Montagne des Louves.
Wiseacres were not surprised—but was this an end or a
beginning? There were old debts to be paid in those backwoods. Fresnes les Puits had indulged in many kinds of
rivalry with St Blaise over the centuries, but for four years
from 1940, the collaborators of Fresnes had made more
indelible marks than the resisters. Charvet, Mayor of
Fresnes, had owned the only *auberge* in the village fit to be
patronized by field-grey officers. Also he had made a sad
miscalculation about who was going to win the war. Like
his masters in Vichy, all he wanted was for France to live
quietly on after the undeniable defeat: and for Les Platanes
to flourish. There had been caustic resentment in Fresnes
of the reprisals that had once or twice been brought down
on the community by things that had gone on in and beyond

Le Baou: Charvet had not been without his supporters in the village—until after the field-grey officers had gone. (Madame Piquemal was Charvet's daughter. She had waited on men in field grey, it was true: but the extent of her collaboration, for which she was held under arrest for weeks by the *Septembristes*, had never gone beyond the slavery of keeping a small hotel alive under difficult conditions. But Fresnes les Puits liked to be unforgiving—even when there was virtually nothing to forgive.)

And in Fresnes this morning, the talk went on.

'It was the Bessons who brought up the child she had.'

'She hasn't been back there since the Liberation. It's taken the grand-daughter's *fiançailles* to bring her back to these parts.'

'Either that's brought her back, or the Englishman has.'

'He was never the father of that child.'

'The way they lived in those camps, who can have known whose man was which?'

Then, seeing that Kenworthy was listening at his corner of the zinc, they retreated into whispering and *patois*. A few theories, at least, were dropping into place.

Later in the morning—indeed, while Kenworthy was crossing the main street—Judge Arribat's Rolls drove in from St Blaise, with the liveried man at the wheel, the Judge and Chantal Dupuy in the rear seat. So that *bruit* was punctured, and Fresnes les Puits had to look elsewhere for hard facts.

It found them when Madame Marini, wife of the butcher, came back on the bus from renewing her Valium prescription at the surgery. It was Madame Ripault who had been found done to death on old Besson's property: the first time in the memory of anyone in this knot of villages that anyone but the woman in nun's grey had opened the doctor's door to them. A cleaning woman was answering the doorbell, and Dr Aubin, thunderously bad-tempered, was having to do his own fetching and carrying.

Yes—there was another who had never been able to keep her fingers out of pies that did not concern her.

'She knew more secrets than any other woman in the *pays*.'

'And she knew how to keep them.'

'Some loads are dangerous to carry.'

'There's a load of dirt to come into the open before they get to the bottom of this.'

Kenworthy hung about and waited. It did not take his practised eye long to notice that he was not the only one who was hanging about. He even spotted when the man's relief arrived, and how they operated the change-over, speaking out of the corners of their mouths over a glass of *Ricard*. Fayard was taking no chances. If there was suddenly a clear need for a hand on Kenworthy's shoulder, he was going to know where Kenworthy's shoulder was. And there were other things. Who had Kenworthy tried to contact? Who tried to contact him? Only when Kenworthy was actually in his bedroom was he actually out of sight of his tail.

How long would it take the examining magistrate to send for him? Kenworthy was looking forward to the interview from several angles. For one thing, he was interested in seeing the system at work from the inside. For another, he hoped for an enlightening hour or so with an official of intelligence, experience and furnace-tempered pragmatism: a cosy picture in Kenworthy's mind of a man in his own mould. After all, the possibility did exist.

In his mind also was an image of Monique Colin. His telephone call to the Agence had had to be succinct, because the landlady was listening to every syllable that went out through the hotel mini-switchboard. And although she was playing almost convincingly at being clandestinely on Kenworthy's side, he did not doubt that she was passing on to Fayard's henchman every word that she thought might bring him pleasure.

'St Hubert.'

'If I might speak to Mademoiselle Colin—'

'Speaking.'

'Kenworthy here. Are you busy?'

'Reasonably.'

'I need help, possibly full-time for a day or two.'

'We could cope with that.'

'I'm in a village called Fresnes les Puits. Do you know where that is?'

'Roughly.'

'I may need a messenger. I'm on the periphery of something that's happened at a holding called Les Carreaux, proprietor Besson, Montagne des Louves. Somebody's been killed. I don't know who. The PJ have matters in hand.'

'Who from the PJ?'

'Fayard.'

There was a pause, for so long that he thought she had gone away—he had heard nothing happen to the line. Perhaps her knowledge of Fayard called for some mental adjustment to the assignment. He pictured her sitting at her typewriter wearing something outrageously unoffice-like, avant-garde and undissemblingly erotic.

'Where are you staying?' she asked him at last.

'The Auberge des Platanes. And perhaps I ought to warn you that this involves a lady not unknown in French twentieth-century history.'

'*Qui ça?*'

'Chantal Dupuy.'

There was an even longer pause than the one that had followed his reference to Fayard.

'This sounds as if it's going to be interesting,' she said at last. 'We'll be in touch.'

That was all. She went out of his life again as untraceably as she had done on the eve of her coup at the airport.

For the rest of the day nothing happened—and the non-event was a slow-burner. He toyed with getting into conversation with Fayard's man, just for devilry, rejected the idea because Fayard's man did not look as if he had the wits to appreciate an ironical situation.

As on an aircraft, meals and a modest drink-programme became cherished landmarks. He had a *croque-monsieur* for his lunch and Madame served him roast leg of lamb for his dinner. The CID man sat playing Napoleon patience at one of the café tables. Kenworthy drank a carafe of Côtes de Provence. Every time the telephone rang he was tempted to leave his chair. The call was never for him.

It was after half past nine that Fayard came in, this time alone. The man playing cards gave no sign of recognizing his master. Was he under the impression that he had got away with his act?

Fayard came straight to Kenworthy's table.

'You've eaten?'

'Excellently, thank you.'

'I've come to drive you to Nice. The magistrate's working overtime. You've completed the statement I asked you for?'

Kenworthy handed it over. Fayard stood and read it, offered no comment.

He drove down the mountain roads at higher speeds than Kenworthy would have done. The hairpins of the *corniche* held no surprises for him. For the first few minutes there was no conversation. Kenworthy did not bother to try. If it suited Fayard's approach to play the sphinx, so be it. Then the PJ Inspector had an unaccountable change of mind, like a pre-occupied dentist who suddenly remembers that he ought to be establishing a relationship with his patient. He started talking about a monumental aqueduct that they could see stretching over the pass, something to do with compensation water from a hydro-electric scheme. Kenworthy summoned up appropriate interest.

'I'm sorry I've had to keep you bogged down all day,' Fayard said. 'Ruining your holiday.'

'Holiday? I can think of better holidays than trying to

mind a man who doesn't want to be minded. Have you found the Colonel, by the way?'

For seconds it seemed as if Fayard was going to retreat into stubborn muteness. But again he stirred himself.

'No. We haven't.'

'Are you in a position yet to give me any idea of what's happened?'

'That will be easier when I know myself.'

The Palais de Justice was all but deserted. A *gardien* in cloak and *képi* stepped up to them as they climbed the steps, recognized Fayard at sight. The spacious entrance hall was silent and institutional: a reception bureau and a Legal Advice *guichet*, glass-fronted, like foremen's offices.

The examining magistrate's office was on an upper floor along a dispiritingly yellow-painted corridor. Even the plaque proclaiming the realm of the *Procureur de la République* seemed somehow less than awe-inspiring. They stopped before a labelled door: Henri Bourjol, *Juge d'Instruction*.

Fayard told Kenworthy to wait, knocked, entered, carrying Kenworthy's statement in his hand. Some time elapsed before he reappeared.

Bourjol had neither the classical culture nor the dried-out competence of Arribat. He was young, Kenworthy would have thought, for the position that he held. He had about him an air of untidy informality: no tie, and his shirt collar open and askew at the throat. Perhaps this spell of overtime was very unofficial indeed. Did *juges d'instruction* ever do anything that was not official? Kenworthy could not dispel the impression that this man rarely let himself look more pompous than he did at this moment.

'Come in, Monsieur Kenworthy. Sit down. We are sorry to make such demands on your time during a rare visit to France. How do you find the nooks and crannies of the Alpes Maritimes?'

'Enigmatic,' Kenworthy said.

'Yes. I can see that.'

Bourjol's fingertips touched the edge of Kenworthy's statement, which lay straightly aligned on the blotter in front of him.

'Thank you for a clear and concise narrative. Not an assignment that will give you much pride when you come across it in your case-book in years to come, I fear.'

'I fear not.'

It was always difficult to be certain about the youngsters that Kenworthy was constantly meeting in high places these days. The slapdash exterior had a habit of hiding a clout of efficiency. You found your affairs were being handled by a youth who could not possibly know what it was all about, and he made sudden spurts, clearing nonsense out of the way. Bourjol would have been on the phone to London this morning, as soon as Fayard had mentioned Kenworthy's name to him.

'Has Inspector Fayard put you in the picture?'

'I think that Inspector Fayard is probably still awaiting your authority to do that.'

'Your Colonel has disappeared into the thin mountain air. The body of an unidentified woman has been found near the impoverished little farm where we would have expected him to have been staying—and where they adamantly deny having seen him for forty years.'

The body of *une inconnue*—

'The villagers believe they know whose body has been found,' Kenworthy said.

'Our hill-villagers may be deprived of some of the century's amenities, but they are never uncertain about anything under the sun. Nor does it ever disconcert them when they are proved wrong. Who do they think she is?'

'They thought at first it was Chantal Dupuy—until they saw her alive.'

'Chantal Dupuy was very highly impressed by you, by

the way, Monsieur Kenworthy. I would say that that is almost without precedent.'

So he had had Mademoiselle in here earlier in the day. This was where she would be coming when she passed through Fresnes les Puits in the Rolls.

'Then they had reason to be convinced that it was Madame Ripault, a doctor's factotum in St Blaise.'

The magistrate looked at Fayard.

'That name is new to me. Could there be a connection?'

'Possibly. Madame Ripault is off duty today, suffering, her doctor insists, from nervous prostration. Our inquiries are not yet complete.'

Bourjol opened the top central drawer of his desk and brought out a dossier. He opened it and passed it over to Kenworthy.

'Here is a morgue photograph of the lady found on the Montagne des Louves.'

Placid features: cleaned up by the pathologist. Looking somewhat older than when Kenworthy had last seen her.

Agnes Neville.

CHAPTER 13

Driving back up under the aqueduct, Fayard appeared to have taken on fresh spirit. Perhaps it was partly because he had seen the *juge d'instruction* treat Kenworthy as an honest man. On a higher loop of the highway a trio of heavy lorries was climbing, equidistant, their engines roaring, lights on their every corner.

'So it's your Colonel's wife who's been killed. I have to ask: it wasn't her husband she'd briefed you to cover, was it? It was herself?'

'No. That's not true. It's been the biggest surprise in my life that she'd come to France herself.'

'Mustn't she have left England almost as soon as Neville did—possibly the same day?'

'If not earlier.'

'She could have done that without his knowledge?'

'I would think so. I don't know anything about the domestic arrangements of the Nevilles. I know nothing about their marital history or their style of life. I spent a very short time in their house—and that was on the ground floor. I could do no more than guess how they got on together.'

'This will mean getting inquiries made in London. This is going to be one of those cases—'

'I can now see through one difficulty that's been worrying me,' Kenworthy said.

Fayard dipped his headlights as they came up behind a slow-moving van.

'What difficulty's that?'

'It's been niggling at my mind ever since I first met Neville in Nice. It was feasible that he had discovered accidentally that his wife had put me on his trail. There are all kinds of ways in which he could have found out. He might have picked up a hint and then bullied her. He talked about screwed-up notes, and a scribble on a telephone pad. But there seemed something just a little too facile about it. He must have had a few days' notice, because he had time to employ the old lady who made an ass of me at the airport. Now I feel certain that he and his wife lived independently of each other at least some of the time. They respected each other's privacy. If one of them wanted to keep something secret, it would have been the easiest thing in the world. Agnes Neville must have been either very stupid or very careless to let Neville know that she had engaged me. And she did not strike me as either a stupid woman or a careless one. Therefore, she wanted him to find out.'

'Why should she want to do that?'

Fayard was not actually being hostile, but it would not take much to make him so.

'To put completely out of his mind any thought that she might be coming to France herself,' Kenworthy said.

Fayard seemed to concentrate fiercely on his steering for a matter of minutes.

'That could make a lot of sense,' he said then.

Fayard came back into the Auberge des Platanes with Kenworthy. He seemed reluctant to go home and to bed, and as they went on talking, Kenworthy could see Madame Piquemal moving about quietly in the background, coming and going between her office and her private quarters. When Fayard finally went, she came over and started a line of small talk, giving Kenworthy the opportunity, if he would, to tell her all that had taken place in the magistrate's office. The last thing on earth he could expect from her was consistency. If one of her residents were under suspicion by the law, she would be no sort of ally. She would make sure that her own front and flanks were covered. Kenworthy did his best to suggest in jocular fashion that he was relieved to be in the clear, but he stemmed her efforts to pry for details. He did not even tell her who it was who had been killed: tomorrow morning would be soon enough for her to start a new range of speculating. She, of course, was highly sensitive to his reluctance to keep her informed, and he knew that under the surface she was bristling. He smiled at her, wished her good night and went up to his room.

The need to be alert all the evening had excited his brain, and he did not feel ready for sleep. He put on pyjamas and dressing-gown and sat down for half an hour of note-making. This usually had the effect of making his eyelids droop.

After ten minutes, he began to feel that it was working. He fell asleep in the middle of a sentence, then jerked awake again, scrabbling for his pen, which had got lost somewhere under the sheets. He was trying to remember how one switched off this particular brand of bedside light when he heard a noise somewhere under his window. It overlooked the rear of the hotel, a mess of empty beer kegs, crates of dead bottles and discarded bits and pieces of hotel furniture. Madame had insisted on giving him this room, assuring him that it was quieter than those at the front of the house.

He hoped that the intruder would be nothing more lethal than a hunting cat, or better still nothing at all. In any strange community there were a thousand night sounds that need not concern him. But this disturbance persisted—and it persisted in giving the impression that it was neither cat nor triviality. These were unmistakably human feet, and he was in no doubt that their focus of interest was his window. Kenworthy got quietly out of bed and studied the best way to approach the window without casting his shadow across the curtain.

Then the footsteps took a walk from the window. There was a minor crash, as if something had fallen from the stacked rubbish of the yard. And after that came the deep, unnatural silence that follows an accidental noise made by an experienced marauder—the freezing into shadow, the holding of breath, the prayer to remain unseen when the expected investigator appears.

No investigator did appear. Kenworthy took up his position on the left of the window, not knowing what he was going to do next. It might have to be something quick and decisive. A space of two minutes passed. He heard the person come out of the shadows. The feet approached and stopped directly under the window. There was another pause. Then something tapped two or three times against the pane, something light but firm—an old curtain-rod, perhaps.

His first hope was that it would be Monique Colin from the Agence, coming to make an interim report. That would certainly scandalize Madame Piquemal—a young lady of Monique Colin's persona seeking him out in his bedroom at this hour. But surely Mademoiselle Colin had not had time yet to come to grips even with the preliminaries. It was doubtful whether she would even have made a start on them yet. Still: she might have turned up for extra briefing.

He put a hand under the curtain and fumbled with a window-fastening of a type that he did not understand, and that behaved as if it had not been opened for a long time. At last the handle turned, and both wings opened inward with more noise than he would have wished for.

A female voice that he did not at first recognize came up at him in a heavily forced whisper.

'Silence! Do not speak!'

For half a minute he stood obediently quiet and still. Then the voice spoke again.

'Monsieur Kenworthy?'

'Oui?'

'Come down through the kitchen. Let me in. *Fâites attention!* Disturb no one!'

Chantal Dupuy.

He could not believe that all this cloak and dagger precaution was necessary. The medium was the message. Here in France, the precautions, it seemed, were more fun than the objective.

He closed the window, put his torch in his dressing-gown pocket, decided that prowling this hotel at night was best done in stockinged feet. There was a *minuterie* on all floors —a system of dim lights that stayed on for rather less than a minute to enable one to get about—and that usually caught one marooned at the maximum distance between switches. He decided against using it. He did not know in which room Madame slept—but he imagined that even if she closed both eyes, one ear would remain active.

He moved towards the head of the staircase, halting now and then to listen for signs that he had alerted anyone. As far as he knew, he was the only guest in the house.

He did not normally react to any sense of the spooky but there was something disturbing about the emptiness of this

hotel. Somewhere in the building someone turned a tap on.
It could surely only be Madame Piquemal at her bedroom
washbasin. He stood back round a corner of landing, waiting
for her door to spring open. It didn't. The running water
seemed to set up a chain reaction throughout the plumbing
of the entire establishment. He waited a minute before
moving again, came down to the ground floor, crossed the
bar-lounge, in which the house cat, an immense neutered
tom, was asleep in a cane chair.

It would be just his luck to find the inner door of the
kitchen locked—but it was actually standing ajar. A red
light was fluttering in a cruciform neon-tube shrine on the
wall. The bolts of the door to the outside world were stiff,
sudden and, when he finally shifted them, created enough
noise to waken the village. There was a chill in the yard,
which seemed utterly deserted. He looked up and saw which
window was his, the only room with lights on. He waited,
and was just coming to the conclusion that whoever it was
who had been here had gone away again when Chantal
Dupuy glided out of a shed doorway and past him into the
kitchen.

'No one knows you've come down?'

'No one.'

'Your landlady mustn't know I've been here. She's the
worst gossip in the Midi—and on everybody's side at one
and the same time. Let's get up to your room. You go first
and I'll follow.'

This must have been the tone in which she had given her
wartime orders to any starving desperado who questioned
her authority. Kenworthy was not concerned with the proto-
col of command. What he most wanted was to put himself
as quickly as possible behind his door again, relatively safe
from the likelihood of an irate nocturnal scene. He made his
way back to his room, uneventfully, but with several stops
to test the silence. Chantal Dupuy seemed a long time
behind him. God knew what she was finding to poke her

nose into in the Auberge des Platanes. At last she arrived, announcing herself by a novelettish scratching on the door-panels.

She looked less greyly formal than when Kenworthy had last seen her, though it was not easily apparent what she had done to her appearance to soften it. A mauve chiffon tied at her neck with long corners hanging? A brooch in the form of a bright green lizard? Perhaps it was a softening of attitude rather than of accessories. Her professional image must have become a habit of mind, after well over thirty years of it. Even the achievements of her outlawish youth had probably as often as not been forced through by a forbidding exterior. Chantal Dupuy could surely never have been a joker. Or one who laughed much at other people's jokes.

She looked disdainfully at the wallpaper and fittings, fingered a threadbare corner of sheet that would have to be discarded before it had bedded many more visitors.

'My God—is this the best she could find for you in an empty house? Does the *Syndicat d'Initiative* recommend this place? I wonder when they last came and inspected it. I'll have to have a word in a few ears.'

'It serves my purpose,' he said. 'I couldn't find a bed in St Blaise.'

He had a fairly good idea what she was here for: an exchange of information. The grapevine would have let her know that he had been taken down to see the *juge d'instruction*, who had had her in earlier in the day. That would have been a tricky interview, with a couple of powerful officials on their guard, anything in the nature of *scandale* anathema to both of them. If the magistrate had the slightest suspicion that she was even indirectly involved in the crime, then it must have been one of the most careful-footed preliminary inquests that he had ever conducted. Now she undoubtedly wanted to find out how Kenworthy had fared with the same official. She would want to know what he had deduced about

the way Fayard's mind was working. She was not exactly
in a nervous state—she was not that sort of woman. But
neither was she the sort of woman who cared for events to
be outside her control—still less outside her knowledge.

'It's time you and I compared notes, Mr Kenworthy.'

He had cleared a disgustingly untidy chair for her, and
had perched himself on a corner of the bottom of his bed.

'I wish I could offer you a spot of decent hospitality,' he
said. 'I've got a few liquid ounces left of what I bought in
the Duty-Free—if you don't mind drinking out of a plastic
mug.'

She made mutterings to the effect that it was a matter of
indifference to her whether she had anything to drink or not
—but she evidently appreciated getting a glass in her hand.

'I can't remember when it was that I last tasted whisky.'

He was taking the opportunity now to study her closely,
without troubling to hide the fact that he was studying her.
It was easier to imagine her putting some poor sod in the
dock through a ruthlessly structured hell than it was to see
her as a dashing improviser in the backwoods. But there
was no doubt that she had been that. He tried to see through
her undeviating orthodoxy to her obliterated youth.

'I know what you are thinking, Mr Kenworthy.'

'I'm not thinking. I'm wondering.'

'Yes. We all wonder. I wondered once about Colonel
Neville. And I'm wondering now about you.'

'You don't wonder about Colonel Neville any more?'

'I don't have to. He isn't my worry any more. He's yours.'

'You were quick enough on his heels when he came out
here after a forty-year gap.'

'That's a long story, Mr Kenworthy.'

'Are you going to tell it me?'

'Not till I know where you really stand.'

'Quite simple. I'm Colonel Neville's guardian, commissioned by Mrs Neville.'

'You still sticking to that?'

'Don't you think it's true, mademoiselle?'

'It could well be. Tell me about Mrs Neville.'

'I know hardly anything about her.'

'You're working for a woman you don't know?'

'That's fairly normal for a private eye, isn't it?'

'A pretty unique kind of private eye, aren't you?'

He understood. It was next to impossible to make a character like Chantal Dupuy believe that he, a fairly senior retired Yard man, was not here on an official brief.

'You think that I'm here on behalf of the powers-that-be?'

She answered him with a look—a look that said she shared with him a close knowledge of the way authority worked; and that he was wasting his time trying to fool her.

'I can do no more than repeat: I'm here to do what I've already told you I'm here to do. I'll swear that on any kind of oath that you care to stipulate. If, that is, you are open to any kind of persuasion. But let's get back to Mrs Neville —or, rather, to Neville.'

Shadow-boxing—because two things had come into his mind. One was that Chantal Dupuy considered it perfectly natural that the British Intelligence Services should still be taking an active interest forty years on from Neville's war-time assignment—enough interest to attach a man to Neville now. It did not seem to surprise her in the least. Therefore she must believe that there were untied ends to that mission that could still be of more than passing interest to governments.

His second thought was: did she know who had been killed? In the next phase of pirouetting dialogue he had to find that out.

'What do you know about Mrs Neville?' he asked her.

'What do you expect me to know about her? Obviously I've never met her. I saw her maiden name in print once— and I don't think I could have told you the day after what it was. I certainly couldn't now. I've had no contact with

Colonel Neville over all these years—and I've never wanted any.'

'But you knew he was coming here.'

'It was certainly neither of the Nevilles who told me.'

'Who, then?'

'I have not come here to be interrogated, Mr Kenworthy.'

'No, you have come, to quote your own phrase, to compare notes. I'm not interrogating you. I am simply indicating where the blanks in my own notebook are. You do know, I take it, that it is the second Mrs Neville that we are talking about?'

'I do know that. That was how I came to see her maiden name in print. A colleague at the bar, who also did some undercover work in the war years, happened to see their wedding notice in the London *Daily Telegraph*. He sent it to me.'

'Did you send them a wedding present?'

Trailing his coat—

'I certainly did not.'

Taking his question entirely seriously—

'I have had no communication of any kind with either of the Nevilles.'

'But you must have had a woman's curiosity as to the sort of second wife he'd have found himself.'

'A passing curiosity. Not strong enough for me to go to any trouble to satisfy it. While he was here before, he talked to me interminably about his first wife, whom he idolized.'

A touch of bitterness? Bitterness on what score?

'I don't even know what happened to his first wife— whether she died, or the marriage broke down,' she said.

'And what sort of picture did you formulate of the second one?'

'None whatever. How can I possibly have formulated a picture of her? And why should I try?'

'I suppose it depends on one's way of thinking about people. Whenever I have a name on my mind, it's always connected to some sort of image—even if it's a vague and totally erroneous one. Maybe your mind does not work like that.'

'This is all very hypothetical, Mr Kenworthy. I don't know what you're trying to lead up to.'

Kenworthy laughed—and Chantal Dupuy resented it.

'What's so hilarious?'

'Nothing, really. I rather used to fancy myself at grilling suspects. I'm glad I never had to try to break you.'

'Am I a suspect, then?'

He was glad to see that she was becoming angry; she might drop her guard.

'I suspect you know who it was who was killed up on the Montagne des Louves.'

'I don't think anybody knows who she was. The examining magistrate did not know. Inspector Fayard had no idea.'

'They know now. I told them. When the *juge d'instruction* showed me their photograph of the body.'

'Who was it?'

'You must have some theory.'

'There was a rumour went round that it was Marguerite Ripault—you know, from the doctor's surgery. But she is in bed with nervous exhaustion. Inspector Fayard has checked on that.'

'We heard the same story here in Fresnes les Puits. Previously, you yourself were supposed to have been the victim. That was generally believed until we saw you drive through in the Rolls.'

'Whose body was it, Mr Kenworthy?'

'The second Mrs Neville.'

He doubted whether she could have acted her surprise. It fell little short of shock.

'How come she was here?'

'That's the question that all the big guns are training on.'

'Did *you* know that she was in France? Had you contacted her? You still insist that you were working for her?'

'I had no idea that she was here. I am completely foxed by what has been going on.'

He thought that she was believing him now; at least, she was tempted to.

'This is serious, Mr Kenworthy.'

The adjective seemed absurdly inappropriate.

'Very serious indeed,' he said. 'Especially for Mrs Neville.'

'Mr Kenworthy—I do not appreciate your sense of humour. I will tell you in a moment why I say it is serious. But first I must ask you a few questions. It is my turn to fill in the blanks in my book.'

He inclined his head, putting himself at her service.

'You were questioned by Inspector Fayard. I've no doubt he wanted to know how you spent your day?'

'He did—and I told him. I told him nothing but the truth.'

'About how you passed the afternoon?'

'I told him I sat it out in Les Tilleuls, reading a novel.'

'And that you saw who drove down the hill out of St Blaise?'

'I told him I saw Monsieur Charles Levaray, in company with Madame Ripault, hiring a car from the garage—and you yourself had previously driven out in the Rolls—with Dr Aubin.'

'You told all this to Fayard?'

'It seemed to me dangerous in the extreme to try to deceive the PJ. I have nothing to lose or gain either way. I stuck to facts—and gave Fayard them all.'

This was obviously bad news to her, but she did not take him to task for it. On the contrary, she remained placid in face of the inevitable.

'It's a pity, but you did right, Mr Kenworthy. It is usually good policy, in an emergency, to tell the truth. But the truth is not going to be very convenient for Levaray, Ripault, Aubin and myself. In the long run, it can't hurt us. It doesn't make us guilty of anything, but it is bound to plant ideas in the head of a single-minded man like Fayard. You do see that?'

'Yes—he's bound to wonder if you were up to no good. He struck me as a good average policeman. But then, I am prejudiced. I like people who are nice to me. He started treating me with respect when the examining magistrate did not order me immediately under lock and key.'

'I hope there's no need for me to assure you that all four of us are innocent?'

'I take that for granted—'

Far from true, but good for international relations—

'But Fayard, I suppose,' he went on, 'would be less likely to assume that? And I suppose, if he digs around, he could find feasible motives for you?'

'Nothing that would stand up in the long run. But it's going to be vexatious, putting it at its lowest level, having Fayard scraping up the past and looking at it through smoked glasses—putting the wrong interpretation on things that are wide open to misunderstanding. Those were years of fragile relationships. Mr Kenworthy, I've decided to tell you a little slice of local history.'

'Another wee noggin?'

'I've made sufficient inroads already on your Scotch—'

'I bought two bottles at Heathrow.'

The dialogue was showing every sign of becoming less brittle.

CHAPTER 14

Chantal Dupuy seemed to become a different individual, once her mind was made up to tell her story: more settled, more human, more feminine. She was a handsome woman —Kenworthy had already determined the adjective—and

when she was not concentrating on rhetoric there was a
serenity about her.

There was a certain artificiality about her opening sen-
tences, as if she had rehearsed this speech.

'I suppose you have a clear picture in your mind, Mr
Kenworthy, of Colonel Neville's arrival in St Blaise. You
had several days of his unrelieved company, and I can't
imagine he is not still talking about it. So you'll have heard
how he floated down over the trees—he could not possibly
have seen any trees, by the way—and how he panicked
when he could see no light from villages, traffic or us—
forgetting in his emotional turbulence that he was still above
the cloud-base. The first time I heard all that, I was a very
sympathique listener. I thought his self-honesty made him a
special kind of man. I was young enough in those days to
prefer my heroes to have souls. Young enough, even, to have
heroes.'

Kenworthy topped up her glass.

'And I suppose you can imagine the clandestine radio
message from London that confirmed that he was coming.
Tante Yvette thanks you for the marzipan. Those were the words
in which they confirmed that the night had come. Our
Marzipan Colonel: the nickname almost stuck, before we
had even set eyes on him. It was I who put a stop to that.
Those broadcasts were monitored. Some sharp pair of ears
might pick up something that they did not even understand
—and that could set a ball rolling that could compromise a
whole network. *Notre petit voisin* was much safer.'

What would she have worn in those days? Kenworthy
came back to thinking of trench-coat and beret.

'So can you see us out on our bicycles? Moonlit mountain
roads, and a runner desperately trying to get to us with
news of tonight's movements of the Milice patrols? The
British Colonel making his perfect landing in his designated
field, where two of us were waiting crouched beneath a
cattle-trough? The scramble to get rid of his parachute? The

pretty girl using her wiles to divert the eyes of a sentry up the road?'

How pretty had Chantal Dupuy been as a young woman? Kenworthy found himself wishing very much that he could see a photograph of her in those days.

'I hope I'm painting it vividly enough for you, Mr Kenworthy.'

'I get the picture.'

'No—you don't. Because it wasn't like that. To begin with the man who was supposed to know the Milice orders for the night hadn't been able to get through to us. And of the seven bicycles we had in the section, only two were fit for the road. Do you know what state civilian bicycles were in in France by that stage of the war? Chains worn so thin that they slid over the cogs like oiled string. Tyres down to the canvas. You judged your bike by the state of the canvas. Not that the soles of our shoes were in much better condition.'

She laughed to herself at the memory of some fiendish machine she had ridden.

'And Colonel Neville did not make the perfect moon-landing. The field in which he touched down was five kilometres outside the perimeter of his dropping-zone. Naturally he had been briefed with alternatives for such a contingency. But he did not carry them out. Because he couldn't. Because he was too badly injured even to stand on his feet, let alone walk.'

'I know. I heard about that. What was the name of the old doctor who looked after him? Bézin?'

Mademoiselle Dupuy looked at him sharply.

'Where did you hear the name Bézin?'

'From Dr Aubin.'

Kenworthy thought that the mention of Bézin's name disturbed her more than it ought to have done. It took her a little while to recover her narrative stride.

'It was his own fault,' she said. 'He was honest with us

about that. And I don't think any the less of any man for being frightened under stress. But Colonel Neville told us his mind had gone blank, and I couldn't help thinking that it would have been better if London had sent us a man whose mind was guaranteed not to go blank. The ground hit him before he knew he was anywhere near it. He had no chance to use what he'd learned in the gym about falling. He made a mess of his right ankle—and you know how recalcitrant ankles can be.'

She was back on form again now.

'I don't want to sound spiteful, Mr Kenworthy, but we soon came to the conclusion that we preferred him when his mind was a blank. There were things we knew about Le Baou and la Montagne—things we knew about France, indeed—which meant that for a lot of the time he simply had to take our orders. He was an important personage. It was our job to keep him in a position to do things that were out of our realm. But for two-thirds of the time, he had to do as he was told. I told you yesterday, on Le Baou, when he started thinking for himself, he became a menace. But of course, immobilized as he was in that field, he had no alternative but to think for himself. His first problem was to dispose of his parachute—and he found no solution to that. He dared not set fire to it, for fear of setting up a beacon. He had nothing to dig with, could find no cover in the field. In the end, he crawled about collecting stones to lay on it, made a very feeble job of that. It was found and reported by the tenant farmer the first thing the next morning, which had the whole neighbourhood buzzing with counter-espionage teams for weeks.'

She looked at her whisky glass, then looked away from it.

'I have to give Colonel Neville his due—he was not without ideas. Some of them—a few—were good. The trouble was, he never seemed to recognize which were the bad ones.'

'They said that of Churchill.'

'He realized the position he was in. He had as little hope of finding us as we had of finding him. There was nothing he could do in the darkness. But at the first glimmer of dawn he crawled towards a plantation and looked for a fallen branch that would serve him as a crutch. He must have been in physical agony as he dragged himself to the nearest small dwelling he could see—an old *mas* occupied by a smallholder's widow. He did not go to the big farm because, he argued, the presence of day-labourers might increase his chances of being denounced. He had a point there, but he chose badly with the smallholding. No: let me be fair, he was virtually without choice. The widow was all nerves and fluster, but finally consented to hide him in one of her barns —then went straight round to a neighbour to take a message to the gendarmes. Fortunately the man who went was loud-mouthed about his errand and was overheard by a *maquisard*. He got a message to me. I drove out to the *mas* in Charles Levaray's old *gazogène* banger and snapped *notre petit voisin* almost from under the noses of the gendarmes. It remains to add that the gendarmes were overworked, they were thin on the ground, they were inefficient—and they were reluctant to get into fights if they could stay out of them. If they hadn't dragged their feet, it would have been all up with Colonel Neville. I took him up to Le Baou. We brought Dr—Bézin—up to see how badly he was hurt.'

She looked again at her whisky. Kenworthy took the bottle over to her.

'You do realize, don't you, that Le Baou was not the Maginot Line? It was a Report Centre, a clearing-house for men arriving at random from all over France. We kept very few there, no one for long. But the place had its advantages as look-out and decoy. And when I speak of the Maquis, don't think of a tensely waiting liberation army—not at this time. It was more like a preliminary muster for a peasants' revolt—and an amateur one at that. Armaments were still minimal. Discipline was sloppy. Food and funds had to be largely stolen. For days on end the menu at La Baou was breakfast: boiled potatoes; lunch: baked potatoes; supper: potato purée. These were not men fighting for France—yet —they were men praying to survive.'

She laughed.

'I must not digress, but when I look back, I can see the irony of it. It has been a great help to me—my practice is in the criminal courts—that I spent my formative years inventing and inspiring felonies on the grand scale of impudence: raids on small Town Halls to steal ration tickets; even a bank break-in—because one needed money to keep men and move them about.'

She turned off the laughter.

'We had to keep our Marzipan Colonel on Le Baou. He had been with us two weeks when we picked up another cryptic message—this time to collect the German that he was to meet. We brought her to Le Baou too. More of her later.'

'One moment—you said *her*—'

'Did Neville not tell you that it was a woman he came here to meet?'

'No—nor did Levaray earlier this evening.'

Her brow had furrowed.

'We'll come back to this. Let me get on. Once, when Le Baou was raided and the raiding-party camped in the ruins for forty-eight hours, we had to leave the pair of them there —in the deepest and most hard to find of the mediæval cellars.'

She was now becoming flushed with story-telling or whisky—or both.

'The truth of the matter is that the men in these Maquis camps were more like prisoners than a training army. Colonel Neville was in many respects a prisoner too—and that did not suit him at all. He could be, he often was, an irresponsible handful. He insisted that as a military man— he called himself a one-man commando—he needed to keep physically at the top of his trim. He needed to exercise his ankle, as soon as it began to mend. He was foolhardy. It was difficult to persuade him to keep his head down. He wandered away sometimes from Le Baou. Sometimes he and his German lady-friend—which by then she was—went for walks in the woods.'

Chantal Dupuy read Kenworthy's thoughts immediately.

'Ah, you are saying to yourself, now she gives herself away. Now everything is falling into place. Now, Mr Kenworthy, you are beginning to see the point of the stories you'll have heard about Chantal Dupuy, all the rumours and knowing looks in St Blaise and Fresnes les Puits. You know all about the easy morals of the brushwood camps. And finally you know about the baby abandoned without feeling, all for the sake of an unfeminine career. Am I right? Isn't that the way your mind is working?'

Up to a point it was—but not at the breathless speed she was suggesting—and certainly not with complacent moral judgement.

'Let me say first that the morals of the Maquis were no looser than anyone else's. Except that for most of the men chance would have been a fine thing. And for a woman the sanctions were appalling. We weren't on the pill in the 1940s. Pregnancy and confinement in a fourteenth-century hole in the ground, perhaps in winter, were vivid thoughts for any woman who wasn't a moron. There were even some men who considered the consequences. I'm not saying that I was lily-white. I'm telling you this because I want you to understand that nothing—nothing I did in those days— was casual.'

'Mademoiselle Dupuy—I am not sitting here as an arbiter.'

No—but he was sitting here as her confessor. How many times in her life had she told it all? Why was it important to her of a sudden to convince him? Because she needed to convince herself? Still?

'So you will ask next how I came to lie down with the Marzipan Colonel, when I can speak of him as I have been speaking of him tonight. Point the first is that I did not see his weaknesses at once—or I saw them as welcome signs of a fighting man's humanity. And I did not see his perfidy until much later. I could not believe in his perfidy when it happened. Point the second is that I was inextricably, biologically and spiritually in love with him. In other words, my mind was temporarily deranged. I think I was in love with him even before he came down through his cloud-base. What was I in love with? What is love? You must not overlook the symbolism of Colonel Neville, for those of us who loved freedom and France—the blue-eyed, steel-souled, unassailable Englishman who had jumped through the sky —giant of integrity, spokesman of the nation that had stood alone against impossible odds. Do you know that throughout the *drôle de guerre* we were being told that the English would fight to the last Frenchman?'

She was speaking now with an intensity that she had kept out of her tone so far.

'Oh yes—and there were other things, too. There was Provence in mid-autumn. Gold tints. Air so serene you could look out over the sea for tens of miles. Rehabilitation walks with him along the woodland paths. It all meant something to an impressionable girl brought up in melancholy Celtic romanticism. I wasn't all that tough in those days: I had to play a rôle, for the sake of the things I believed in. I had to be double tough precisely because I wasn't tough. And a well-disciplined gentleman from Sandhurst wasn't unsusceptible to the environment, either. Did I say disciplined? Well, yes—I suppose he was. That might have been one of the things that was wrong with him.'

She reverted to the lower-key drama of her narrative.

'After three years of Occupation, even the most liberal-minded among us weren't happy about risking our lives to bring a Hun through our channels. Some were more outspoken about it than others. One of my hardest tasks was to try to keep them all persuaded that London knew what they were doing. I knew that I might find myself having to protect Horst Molling against some of our own recruits.'

She permitted herself a sardonic twist of the lip.

'Horst Molling. How many wheels within wheels within wheels were there? A supposed *Wehrmacht* deserter from a Signals Unit in Paris, trying to get us to talk London into giving status and infrastructure to a group of undercover dissidents. They claimed they'd support the inevitable Invasion in no end of ways. I met him at Nice main station —off a very crowded, long-overdue train. We were an age inching through the controls, but his papers turned out to be in order. I shall never forget my relief when he was through the barrier. I couldn't help being surprised by the freshness of his face, the softness of his complexion. He did not look like a young man who had ratted out of the *Wehrmacht* and was supposed to have been living rough in the deep country. But the object of the exercise was for Colonel Neville to make an assessment of him as a potential agent. London claimed to be open-minded, to be relying implicitly on his report. The Colonel had an exhaustive schema of questions to put to him, to establish his bona fides —his background, what he had to say about personalities in his home town, army officers: anything that might trip him up. If the Colonel struck an anomaly, then Horst Molling was going to get the hot potato treatment. And it was part of my rôle to act as back-up to the Colonel in all this. I was to supply the feminine intuition, to scan Horst Molling with a woman's eye.'

For a moment her contempt for Neville seemed bottomless.

'I pushed my suspicions under the surface at first. I had to concentrate on the highly dangerous business of getting away from Nice station with a clean-faced young German in civilian clothes. I got him to Le Baou. He had not been with us among the ruins long before more than one man became suspicious. By next morning half a dozen people had taken me on one side, expressing doubts about the German's sex. Had I noticed—? Did I *know*—? The only one who didn't come to me talking behind the back of his hand was Colonel Neville himself. But then, of course, he did know. He had known all along. I challenged him, and he said of course there were women in the German army as well as men: cipher clerks, telex operators. Some of them knew as much as the generals. They often knew things before the generals did.'

She stopped talking to prick up her ears—and Kenworthy had heard the same sound: somewhere in the *auberge* a telephone was ringing. It went on ringing for a long time. Then they heard footsteps over their heads. It must have been ringing at Madame Piquemal's bedside. They heard her bedroom door open. They heard her go down to the ground-floor in the lift: presumably to her office switchboard: the only way in which she could transfer the call. Seconds later, Kenworthy's phone rang.

'*C'est pour vous, Monsieur Kenworthy.*'

CHAPTER 15

'That,' Kenworthy said, 'was my wife.'

'At three in the morning? She must miss you.'

'Oh, she does. And vice versa. She rang because Mrs Neville's daughter has been in touch with her. Interpol had got through about what has happened to her mother. It seems she knew that Mrs Neville was employing me.'

'And Mrs Kenworthy knew how to get hold of you? She knows that you are here at Les Platanes?'

'No. But over the years she has become very adept at

finding me. She still knows a few names and voices at Scotland Yard, and even in the middle of the night she persuaded somebody to contact the Nice *Police Judiciaire*. They knew where I was.'

'It was so very important?'

'She thought so. And so do I, come to that.'

'Don't tell me,' she said. 'I know. Let me tell you first.'

She could bring a formidably high intelligence into play. Besides, she had had the benefit of hearing half the telephone conversation. There was one vital thing that Elspeth had learned from Agnes Neville's daughter. Chantal Dupuy had gone through to it like a wire through cheese.

'No, please don't tell me, Mr Kenworthy. I must be the first to say it. Because I told you a lie earlier tonight.'

'I know you did.'

'I promise you, I had made up my mind to correct it before we finished talking. I told you less than the truth before I was sure I could trust you.'

'And now you think that you can?'

'Mr Kenworthy—how could I have known anything about you before tonight?'

Kenworthy remained noncommittal.

'The second Mrs Neville,' Mademoiselle Dupuy said, 'was one of the executive officers at the headquarters that directed Colonel Neville's mission. She was not very old— on or just above the twenty mark. But she came from the class—we have them too—that expects to step into key roles—and that wears responsibility lightly. It goes without saying that she had no part in shaping policy, or in drafting his orders. Under the usual rules, she was not even supposed to know the reason for his journey. Unofficially, she was bound to. In the normal run of her work she saw his documentation. You will understand that we had many hours together, Rawdon Neville and I, talking about everything under the sun—before I went to Nice to fetch Horst Molling. Agnes Strafford, as she then was, was responsible

for all the practical details of his mission: for getting him
kitted out, for his back-up, for the channels of communication if he needed to send an emergency message. Junior
Commander, that was her rank. I remembered her name
when I saw the cutting from the *Telegraph*. She had waited
years for him.'

'But did she get to hear about all that went on on Le
Baou?'

'She knew what his work was all about, which was more
than I did. More than I do yet. Like the German cipher
clerks we were talking about, she sometimes saw messages
before the General Staff did. So if she came out here, having
deviously employed you so as to pull the wool over her
husband's eyes—well, as I said not long ago—it's a serious
matter.'

'And you felt it necessary to keep this piece of information
from me?'

'There were some things that happened on Le Baou that
none of us were proud of, Mr Kenworthy. Seen within their
context they may not perhaps be all that dreadful. But we
don't want them hawked about in public by people who
could never possibly understand that context.'

Kenworthy did not find this nearly far-reaching enough.
But Chantal Dupuy evidently expected him to, so he let it
go for the time being. He asked her what she knew about
the first Mrs Neville.

'He talked to me a lot at first about his dear Lavinia. He
had obviously projected her on to all the planes where he
wanted her—but he did not really believe it. I remember
thinking at the time, she was the sort of woman who is
married by career officers the world over: the younger sister
of his first adjutant. He was aching to tell me her short-
comings—aching to admit them to himself. That, of course,
was in the second stage of our relationship.'

She smiled whimsically, principally for her own benefit.

'It's no use claiming that I can speak with authority of

notre petit voisin as a lover. He may have improved with the passage of time.'

'Hung up, was he?'

'Very English, I'd say. But that's based on second-hand opinions of your compatriots, and probably most unfair. I remember feeling sorry for his wife—as well as for him. Do you mind if I spare us both a run-down of detail? Passion *à la belle étoile*—something both parties urgently needed under the Provençal sky. Nothing happened until the middle of the third week. So it wasn't a long partnership. Oh yes, it did continue at first—with agonizingly heavy secrecy—after the advent of Horst Molling. Then came the day when Le Baou was raided. We saw them coming and a picket took possession of the hillside for a few days. We dispersed—we were, after all, only a skeleton camp staff. There was this one particular cellar that was as impregnable as Levaray and his regulars had been able to make it: he had been a sapper officer. We hid Neville and the woman down there. Neville was still not mobile enough for speed and distance, and we didn't want the German with us—there were some in the group who wouldn't have trusted her a centimetre, and she would have been a liability if we had run into trouble. When we came back, I didn't doubt what had happened. Do you believe me when I say that a woman can tell at sight that the man she loves has been sleeping with somebody else? She is especially sensitive when she is closeted in close quarters with them. I suppose I even tried to tell myself, as a rational being, not to take it too much to heart. I remember asking myself if he'd made as clumsy a job of it with her as he had with me. Do you know that the wretch even had the nerve to tell me that it was the image of the little woman at home that kept coming between us?'

She had not lost her disgust yet.

'We'd left them alone, making the best they could of a confined space. What could I expect to happen? But when I took him aside and faced him with it, he was cavalier

about it. That was what finished me. He told me we were
both soldiers. This was wartime. Ships passed in the night.
Surely in the walk of life I'd chosen to follow for the last
three years I'd learned that permanent attachments just
wouldn't do? I didn't tell him my currently expected period
was now pretty well past hope.'

'You never did tell him about the baby?'

'I never made any effort to get in touch with him again
after we finally saw him off on his trawler. And he made no
effort to get in touch with me. And here comes the part
that I don't expect you to understand. How can a woman
abandon a child that she has carried for the nine most
dangerous months of her life? Was Chantal Dupuy utterly
devoid of maternal instincts? Should she not love the thing
that she expels in agony from her body, no matter who
planted it there?'

She was not being hysterical, but she could hardly have
been more bitter at the time.

'Don't you think that the converse might also be possible?
Might she not hate the creature of her body, because of the
blood that she knows is bred into it? And it wasn't only
because of a German woman's victory in love that I felt
bitter. There was another discovery I was still to make.
There were other occasions when we had to leave the pair
alone together. It happened increasingly often, in fact, when
Neville could get about more. We all had work to do that
took us away from Le Baou now and then, and the least we
could ask them to do was to share the camp watch and
chores. Once when we'd left them, Le Baou was visited by
a routine Boche patrol. Neville and the woman had ample
time to get themselves lost in the landscape. You remember
the layout of that hill? They had at least seven clear minutes
to get themselves lost in one of the side-valleys. We had
taught them a drill, practised them in it. But this was one
of those days when Colonel Neville had ideas of his own.
This was the day when he laid his trail of blood-spattered

articles of clothing—then vanished in another direction. Even we had no clue where they had gone. Incidentally, it led the Boche to believe that the Vittorinis had harboured them.'

Neville and the girl had headed northwards into a mountain wilderness, a pre-Alpine range whose desolation contrasted with the softer foothills round St Blaise. It seemed that he had been given in London, as special back-up in case of dire emergency, the name of a French industrialist who had a holiday home in one of the more remote valleys. This man was not a member of any organization known to the St Blaise Maquis. He was one of London's reserves—a clinical case of left-hand-right-hand. Neville and the girl found themselves in a boulder-strewn cul-de-sac ravine on the southern flank of the desolate Montagne des Louves. Here they discovered an eccentric tycoon's holiday retreat. It was an eagle's nest folly, unapproachable except by mule-track. It was unoccupied and in a bad state of disrepair. The couple lagered up there for the remainder of that day and the night that followed. When they eventually returned to base, Neville was full of self-justification. The place offered all the security that a fugitive could demand. It commanded a sweeping view of the valley below, surely the way by which any search-party would come. How efficient had been their round-the-clock watch, Neville did not specify. They had obviously found other things to do with at least some of their time and not all their waking hours had been spent scanning the approaches.

It was fortunate that no search-party showed up. Neville's only armament was a small-calibre Erboa automatic, somebody's relic of the Spanish Civil War, for which he had twenty-five rounds. It could have done no damage except at very close range. And for food they were even worse off, reserves on Le Baou being at one of their lowest ebbs. They took with them a day's supply of stale bread and one small lump of dry, unpalatable cheese. And the sole contents of the larder in their eyrie was one pre-war tin of pineapple chunks—which they considered extremely funny when they came to describe the meal they had made of it. Short commons, Neville called it.

Chantal Dupuy told Neville that the grand strategy of his assignment was his affair, but that unless he submitted without reservation to her absolute command in all local tactical matters, she proposed to get a message to London that she could not take further responsibility for him. This would have been a desperate throw. She doubted whether she would ever have carried it out—it was a round that she knew she was more likely to lose than to win.

But Neville was contrite. He admitted that she was right. He repeated that they were both soldiers, and that each must reign supreme in their allocated department. It looked as if the air had been cleared—as far as concerned military matters. The disciplinary issue was settled, the immediate tactical future assured. Chantal Dupuy steered clear of personal comment. But there was a worse confrontation to come.

There was one occasional visitor to Le Baou, a man called Combret, a former telephone engineer from Dijon, who came and went as liaison officer to outlying contingents. He was better educated than the general run of the *maquisards*, was something of a political firebrand, and had lost patience with waiting games. One day Combret had found himself by chance eavesdropping on Neville and the German woman. He understood German and came to Mademoiselle Dupuy with what he had heard. And when she appeared to be dragging her feet about it, he had no inhibitions about enraging his companions with the story. The ensuing unrest compelled her to act. She had to have another discussion with Neville off-stage.

'*Mon Colonel*, you owe me an explanation about the nature of the business you are transacting with Fräulein Fischer.'

'I owe explanations to no one, Chantal. We had this out

the other day. We each have our own sphere of activity. We can only co-exist if we both respect that.'

'I'm sorry—but you have been appallingly indiscreet, *mon Colonel*. It is only a matter of days before this will be common talk in every one of our encampments. It seems that this story about a knot of deserters from the German army is nothing but a blind.'

What Combret had overheard had been an interchange between an industrial concern in England and a complex of factories, the *Fischer Haurath Betrieb, GmbH*, on the outskirts of Ludwigshafen. One was the parent company of the other; Chantal Dupuy had not been clear which was which. But it seemed that in peacetime a third of the directors of the German company were British nominees, though not necessarily themselves British. There were contractual agreements for the exchange of technical information, and it had sounded to Combret as if these were being invoked even in midstream of total war.

It had been common talk in the 'twenties and 'thirties that there had been similar instances during the First World War—understandings about not shelling certain factories behind the lines. Their post-war prosperity must not be jeopardized. It was more than Chantal could stomach that this should be happening again—that the book-keeping of the wealthy should be above the ideologies for which some people thought they were fighting this war. It seemed that high finance—which when reduced to its constituent terms meant the finance of individuals—could even manipulate the resources of the British War Office. And French freedom-fighters were losing their lives for it.

Neville's first response was a strenuous denial.

'It was pathetic, Mr Kenworthy. I had to quote verbatim some of the things that Combret had heard. And he tried to laugh those off as misunderstandings, said Combret was a man of pretty dull mentality, anyway—though as far as I know they had never talked for long together. He also took exception to having been spied on. I told him a few home-truths. He was not lording it now over a barracks where discipline was supported by a traditional system. He was working with men—and women—whom he could only control by persuasion and respect. At this point he obliquely admitted that there was a trace of substance in Combret's allegations. But the ultimate could not be told for reasons of highest level secrecy: it was far removed from what I was thinking. He was wholly unconvincing. I have seen men in the dock fall back on that sort of indignant nonsense. There were things going on that could not come to light until the end of the war. It would be highly injurious to the Allied cause if this matter did come to be talked about in the camps. He must rely on me to scotch these rumours, to issue an authoritative denial, to discipline Combret, to forbid uninformed speculation in my ranks.'

Then Fräulein Fischer was murdered. There was no doubt that it was murder. She was found a few metres beyond the perimeter of Le Baou with her cervical vertebrae dislocated from behind.

'Everybody was suspect and I was the favourite. Nine-tenths of the *maquisards* thought it was a vengeance killing for stealing *notre petit voisin*'s affections. My private belief was that Combret had done it: one problem at least that he had been able to liquidate with his own hands. But it might have been anyone who had views of his own about extending hospitality to dubious Boches. I was anxious about losing an agent whom we were supposed to be controlling. There was little sympathy for me. Germans killed in France in 1943 were not generally mourned. Except this one—by Colonel Neville. He was very untalkative for the remainder of his stay.'

Tell François that Gabrielle's fourth pigeon has arrived—

That was the signal that Neville was to start for home. The word *fourth* fixed the date. They smuggled him aboard a trawler that was to draw another wake of misery and grief.

An outpost perched on a rock above Garavan kept an eye on that boat through binoculars to make sure that she did not sail without him. And that was the only send-off that Colonel Rawdon Neville had from the secret fighters of Le Baou. Chantal Dupuy left the Riviera that same night. She had lost any taste she had ever had for Mediterranean palms and the splendours of the Alpes Maritimes. There were threads for her to pick up afresh in Brittany, problems that would not have cropped up there but for her absence. She threw herself at the menace of death, hoping that it would be so sudden when it came that she would not notice.

CHAPTER 16

'But why did old Plato tell me none of this?'

'Because he is approaching second childhood.'

'You wouldn't accept that answer in any of your courts.'

She looked at him peculiarly. Had advocacy reduced her to the state where civil conversation was a series of points lost or won? And then she softened her attitude. Was it only because she thought she ought to soften it?

'You're right. I shouldn't have said second childhood. Charles has had only one childhood. It's lasted all his life.'

She smiled, but not warmingly. Again, it might have been because she thought she should.

'One of my secondary roles in '43 was to report on the state of things here in the field. I had to recommend that they get rid of Levaray. Actually, they shunted him somewhere where he hadn't to be relied on. He was an officer whose career meant everything to him: a career that had lasted a matter of months. His total experience was ineffectual—not entirely his fault, in the retreat of 1940. But he was stiff, had neither imagination nor initiative, was scared of innovation, couldn't make decisions without the full

back-up of the system. He passionately admired your
Colonel. Need I say more? We had many differences of
opinion on Le Baou, and I had given up consulting him. I
certainly held no discussion with him on the subject of
Fräulein Fischer. And when she was murdered, he said flatly
that in any post-war commission of inquiry—he went in
perpetual fear of post-war commissions of inquiry—his defence would be that the basic facts about Fräulein Fischer's
had been kept from him. So it sounds to me as if he's sticking
to that thesis now. He thinks the vanguard of the post-war
commission has arrived at last. You, the former Yard man,
are it. So he's gone back to where he was when he first heard
that a young man called Horst Molling was coming. Can
you think of anything more pathetic?'

Chantal Dupuy had no margin of time or occupation in
which to trouble herself about post mortems after the war.
She told Kenworthy how she finally gave up hope of losing
her baby. She had prayed that exertion, fatigue, suspense
and terror would loosen that embryo from the walls of her
womb. She would take her chance of being rescued, soaked
in her own blood and mucus, from some quayside, some
gutter or railway goods-siding. You couldn't speak of
bravery, she told Kenworthy, when you no longer cared
what anybody did to you. Sabotage in shunting-yards;
landing-lights for moondrops more efficient than Neville's;
traffic-signs transplanted to wreak havoc when Nazi ar-
moured divisions changed station. And her baby held obsti-
nately on. She wanted nothing to do with abortion, amateur
or underground professional. Perhaps, she added, twisting
a knife inside herself, that was her last lingering genetic
memory of maternal feeling.

It began to seem that she might be going to be spared to
have a future. That needed thought—but there was no
drawn-out conflict. She came to a conclusion on one particular night, effacing herself for three hours on the water-front
at Brest. The war was going to be over soon—for those who

survived. She was alone on a wharf where it was a capital offence to be. It was a chance for tormented thinking—she who had had any woman's fill of tormented thinking. There were whole regiments of women in her position—and that thought brought her no pleasure. She never had cared for being faceless in any crowd. It was time to make her decision. And once it was made, that had to be the end of tortured thinking.

Her future had to be a professional career. It had to be independence. There could be no question of harnessing herself to mediocrity for the rest of her life—and certainly not for the sake of a creature that she was likely to hate even more as a reality than she did now as a notion.

There was a family in the hinterland of St Blaise—the Bessons, who subsistence-farmed on the Montagne des Louves. She knew they would spare nothing to help her. They were convinced, Marie-Claude Besson particularly, that they owed her a cosmically enduring debt—it had to do with a brother she had had spirited away from the departure platform of a Rhine-bound train. She knew that the Bessons wanted to adopt a child: they had said they were going to as soon as the war was over. She had acted as a sounding-board, encouraged them to talk about the risks and difficulties of taking an unknown heredity. Well —here was a child as 'safe' as any they might find. She would create generous initial financial foundations, even if it left her present savings account empty. She made generous promises for the future, on none of which she had ever reneged. Indeed, there was to come a time when she could send unheard-of funds to the Bessons without missing them.

'You've seen my brainless grandchild about St Blaise, Mr Kenworthy. The day I took you to Le Baou, she passed us in the car with her gallant nobody of a fiancé. She smiled at you, didn't she, on the weight of knowing who you are? Oh, she is innocent and harmless. A doll. The prettiest of babies. What fun I could have had, couldn't I, taking her under my wing—hauling her off for a bottom-drawer shopping spree in the glossy new *Etoile* at Nice?'

'She seems very well liked in the village,' Kenworthy said.

'In Les Tilleuls, you mean? She would be, wouldn't she? All the world loves a lover. And perhaps you'll have gathered that the wedding is already planned down to the choice of hors d'oeuvres? It's going to be the greatest event in St Blaise since the Liberation—perhaps even since the hanging of Joseph Vittorini. She belongs to everybody. Especially since they all fancy she's about to be transformed into a well-heeled princess, like some child in a fairy story.'

'Did you ever have anything to do with your daughter?' Kenworthy asked her.

'No. Though I can tell you that I was fool enough to feel tempted now and then. I'm glad I withstood that—but she's never forgiven me for anything. Why should she? But I wouldn't have done her any kindness by stirring things up. I left her to the Bessons. That's how they wanted it. They are splendid people—splendid, ordinary people.'

'Did your daughter know as a child who her mother was?'

'We agreed that she was not to be told. That is the sort of clause that is put in a contract by a clever, legally-minded young woman who knows about everything except how splendid, ordinary people live. My God—I thought in those days that I had learned everything there was to be learned. Everyone in this leg of the mountains knew who she was. How could she escape being told? She grew up, married a naval design engineer, went to live in Toulon. Sometimes the family came on camping holidays in the hills. Yvette was taken to meet the Bessons, loved them, and they were enraptured by her. She fell in love with this lad from the garage and now spends as much time as she can near him. Then she wrote to her grandfather, telling him about herself and the forthcoming wedding. Would he help? I expect her mother put her up to it. He wrote to say he would come. The Bessons thought they ought to keep me posted. So you see, it looks as if *Grand-père* has a conscience, even if *Grand'mère* never did.'

She was making no effort now to restrain her bitterness.

'Oh, I can imagine: this was the sort of pomposity that really would appeal to his sense of honour. He talked like that in the old days, about the job he had come to Le Baou to do. And he's clearly grown an even bigger fool with age. And his wife was out here on his heels in a hurry, wasn't she? I'm sure that Agnes Neville's sense of honour would not rise to sacrificing a centime of her inheritance—or her daughter's. I only hope—'

She was only hoping, as was Kenworthy, that splendid, ordinary people had not lost their heads. It was surprising what people would do, when they thought they could get away with it. Murder for sordid gain had happened before —and not only in remote French peasant regions.

'How old are these Bessons?'

'My age—our age.'

'And you don't think—?'

'I'd say I'm as sure of their morality as I am of anyone I know.'

'It was near their place that Mrs Neville's body was found, wasn't it? What was the name of their farm? Les Carreaux—'

'She'd have gone there because it was the only likely address in the locality that she knew. It would have been from there that Yvette would have written to her husband.'

'There is one important thing I'd like to ask you.'

'Thank goodness you are behaving like a policeman at last. I can guess what you're wanting to know. Where were we all going yesterday afternoon, while you sat reading your book? We were going to look for Rawdon Neville.'

'All of you? Why Dr Aubin, for example?'

'I needed company. I wanted somebody alongside who was strong and uninvolved.'

'So you know Dr Aubin?'

'We have met.'

'Even though he was not in the district in the autumn of 1943?'

'What makes you say that?'

'He told me so himself. As a medical student on the run, he was serving as an irregular MO in the Franche-Comté. That was why Dr Bézin attended to Colonel Neville.'

It was not by accident that Kenworthy mentioned Bézin: he remembered how the name had affected her once before. This time she did not let herself be thrown off balance. She might have been trying to stare Kenworthy out.

'Dr Aubin is a native of St Blaise. He slipped back down here from time to time, even in those years.'

She was a woman trying to sound casual, when what she was saying concealed something of the truth. She was giving an answer that she had not had the time to think out properly.

'So Dr Aubin did meet Colonel Neville here?'

'I can't remember whether he did or he didn't.'

That was feeble. Of course she would remember.

'Well—how would I remember?' she said, condemning herself by over-emphasis, and by answering a question that she had not been asked. 'I was not on Le Baou all the time. He could have come and gone without my knowledge.'

'I'm sorry, Mademoiselle Dupuy—but I think you are being less than open with me.'

'I cannot deny that. I am being anything but open with you.'

'Why?'

'Because others are concerned, besides myself. And what concerns us has nothing to do with the killing of Mrs Neville.'

Kenworthy shrugged his shoulders.

'That's between you and the examining magistrate, then. It has nothing to do with me, either. But yesterday afternoon: did you find Colonel Neville?'

'No, we did not. He was not in the obvious place where we went to look.'

'And that was?'

'On the Montagne des Louves, the opposite flank from Les Carreaux—where he had once made the most of an eagle's-crag love-nest in a decaying summer residence.'

'Is it a place that I can find fairly easily?'

'If you want to. I can give you precise instructions. But you are likely to find yourself tangling with Inspector Fayard if he finds you meddling.'

'I'll take a chance on that. I think Fayard might appreciate my brand of curiosity.'

She left fairly soon after that. On the verge of going, she had again become a worried woman. She said that there was no necessity for Kenworthy to come downstairs with her, but he reminded her that he would have to lock and bolt the kitchen door after her—the sort of point which she would have jumped smartly on herself, if she had not been so preoccupied.

Kenworthy stepped out into the *auberge* yard with her. There were signs that the earliest morning life of Fresnes les Puits was starting up: tyres on the main road, the baker's shutters going up, a dustcart beginning its rounds. Kenworthy went as far as the street-front of the inn. There were already working men drinking espresso coffee in a dingily lit café. Chantal Dupuy turned and waved to him as she disappeared.

Then three cars came into Fresnes along the Nice road. In the first Fayard was being driven by his pachyderm sergeant. The other two were keeping convoy distance. Round the first corner out of Fresnes, Kenworthy heard Fayard pull up. That would be abreast of Mademoiselle. They did a U-turn and came back through Fresnes. The rest of the convoy went on towards St Blaise.

CHAPTER 17

When Kenworthy took a walk along the main street of Fresnes les Puits, he saw that he was now well and truly nailed down here. There was a lounger at either end of the street who did not belong to the community; he knew most of the faces of Fresnes by now. He went to the small business premises that advertised a taxi for hire and was given confused excuses for there not being one available. He rang the garage in St Blaise, and was told that all their cars were out on long-distance runs. It was likely that the young bridegroom-to-be, with his lady love, Chantal, Dr Aubin, Madame Ripault and Levaray were all in Nice by now, immobilized for prolonged and patient statement-taking.

With Agnes Neville dead he had no further commitment. He was likely to be treated unceremoniously by Fayard and the *juge d'instruction* if he was caught prying. Indeed, with a double escort who were not even troubling to conceal themselves, it was difficult to see a way to pry. Yet Kenworthy continued to look for one.

He did not doubt where Neville was; Chantal Dupuy had not doubted that. He was in or near his eagle's nest, where he had shared a wartime tin of pineapple chunks with his German contact. And Kenworthy believed that that was a piece of information that Chantal and her companions would keep from the ears of the magistrate and the PJ for as long as they could; because Dupuy, Aubin, Levaray and Company had things to settle among themselves that did not concern present-day authority.

The cafés of Fresnes les Puits were uninviting, but the morning was still too chilly for sitting about the *pétanque* terraces. He stood at a scruffy counter and drank a cup of thick strong coffee that he did not want and did not like. Outside he could see one of his shadows. Presumably his mate had gone round to keep the rear of the premises covered. And then he saw something that showed him an outside chance of a way out. Past the window of the café drove the hospital service van in which he had had an uncomfortable ride.

An outside chance: Dr Auguste Boillot. He finished his coffee, went out on to the pavement, elaborately ignoring the sleuth, and walked up out of the village to the Tanguy crossroads from which the road to the hospital forked. He took his time, stopped once to relight his pipe, turned in the wind to shelter the flame and assure himself that his escort was still with him. Both men were now on the job, on either side of the road, one thirty yards back and one fifty.

He turned into the hospital drive, went straight to Boillot's office and asked for the doctor. Once the office door was closed behind him, he was out of sight of Fayard's strong-arms.

Boillot came at last, again in a white overall lightly blood-stained, giving the impression that he had again come direct from the theatre. He perched himself on the corner of a desk and looked at Kenworthy with the gorilla-like features that Kenworthy had quickly recognized as sympathetic.

It was tricky. Kenworthy did not know where Boillot fitted into the picture. He did not know how much it was safe to tell him.

'Dr Boillot—I don't know whether you are abreast of what has happened to Madame Ripault and her friends.'

'I know that a compatriot of yours, by coming here, has precipitated something that it would have been better to have allowed to die its natural death.'

Was he holding Kenworthy equally to blame?

'Nevertheless, he came,' Kenworthy said. 'The man is what we in England commonly call a clot. He has been a clot all his life. He has a habit of clotting up everything about him.'

'You express it economically, Monsieur Kenworthy. Things happened in the past, some by impulse, some by mistake, that cannot be changed. But they could have been ignored. I believe in applying a kind of euthanasia to that sort of history—not in reviving it.'

'I am not here to revive it. I came as a bodyguard, hired by the woman who was found dead yesterday on the Montagne des Louves. The Colonel's second wife.'

'That's who it was? Then she was here to—'

'I can only think, to prevent her husband from giving half his fortune—or more—to his grand-daughter as her dowry.'

'There would be no injustice in that,' Boillot said.

'Dare I ask, Doctor, where you fit into this jigsaw?'

'Just think of me as a friend of the family,' Boillot said and did not elaborate on what he meant by *family*. 'So what do you want me to do for you?'

'Help me to throw off two tails from the PJ who are cramping my style. Enable me to get to a mountain villa at which Colonel Neville once lagered up.'

'And why should I do that? So that even more muck can be turned over?'

'No—because I need a private parley with Colonel Neville. The sooner I get him home, the better.'

'I can see that that might serve a useful purpose. But surely there are plenty of other people who could get you there?'

'I believe that Chantal Dupuy, Dr Aubin, Charles Levaray—all the survivors of the old team from Le Baou—have been hobbled by the magistrature and the *Police Judiciaire*.'

'Which means they're going to spend several frustrated hours sitting about in dusty ante-rooms. And you want to get to *notre petit voisin* without delay?'

'If I am right about where he is.'

'You won't know if you don't go and look. These hoods from the PJ—where are they now?'

'They followed me in. At least one of them will be waiting for me to re-emerge through that door.'

'Then you won't re-emerge. I see no difficulty in getting you out of this.'

He left Kenworthy alone and when he came back, led him into the region of wards and technical services. He took him into a vacant consulting room.

'From now on, you are a stretcher-case. There's no need for you to undress—you'll be well blanketed, and while you're still in the hospital, we'll keep your face covered as if you were on your way to the mortuary. If your undetachable friends came asking for you, I shall say you came in complaining of pains that we have diagnosed as mild renal colic and that we have discharged you as a sitting ambulance case, which is how they must have come to miss your exit.'

'Thank you, Doctor—'

'In exchange for all this, Monsieur Kenworthy, I want your promise that you will kill the past. Can I rely on you to do that? You have no axe to grind—get the axes out of everyone else's hands.'

So it was in fact not as a sitting case that Kenworthy was transported out of the hospital, but with the full treatment of uniformed attendants, to complete appearances, a not uncomely nurse to sit with him: the entire hospital seemed to dance to Boillot's tunes. Not until they had driven some five miles out of Fresnes did the nurse pull the sheet away from his face.

'You can relax now. I don't know what any of this is about, but I can think of less restful ways of spending my morning.'

'Are we being followed?'

'*Mon Dieu!* this is like a script for a B film. Are there any Emmies on offer?'

She slid a panel to talk to the driver.

'He says the road behind's been clear for the last ten minutes.'

They turned presently into an unmetalled track that led up away from the highway at an alarming angle and over an execrable surface, rounding hairpins that could only be negotiated by reversing through three-point turns. Then they came to the handiwork of a tree-felling party who had abandoned a giant across their fairway. They came to a halt.

'This is as far as we can make it,' the driver said. 'They're not going to get this cleared today. Shanks's pony for you, my old friend. Know how to get to where you're going?'

'No.'

'Well—I can't help you, mate. I don't know what any of this is about. My instructions were to take you as far as the *Carrefour aux Mélèzes*. That's about another three and a half kilometres uphill. After that, I expect you'll have to think of something.'

It was uncomfortable walking over a sharp-stoned surface, but at least he could set his own speed. There was a pleasant tang of clean soil and pine-resin and every now and then beams of sunshine slanted in, growing warmer as the morning advanced. He did not know that *mélèze* meant *larch*, and in any case would not have recognized a larch if he had been leaning against one. Not once since the fallen tree had he seen any sign of humanity. Finally he reached an intersection of several tracks that looked more important than any other he had come across, sat on a stone to smoke, rest and hope for help or inspiration.

For ten more minutes none came. He tried to persuade himself that it did not matter all that much. He was on a self-imposed assignment that was probably going to get nobody anywhere. He did not even know for certain that Neville would be in his eagle's nest. He had the choice here of four ways, not counting the one by which he had come. Every step along the wrong one would double the distance that he had ultimately to cover. He had no food, no water, no map—and the nearest next-door neighbour was miles away. He had no sort of a grip on anything.

Then he heard a shot somewhere in the distance below him. It was a shot, he told himself, that would have told some detectives something. They would have known whether it was cartridge or ball, pistol or long barrel, rifle or smooth-bore. Without hearing it again, Kenworthy could learn nothing from it. There was some sort of echo, then even that died. There was no follow-up of panicky wings or scurrying small mammals: it was too far away for that. But Kenworthy set off in the direction of that shot. Even if it was only a naïve and amiable Arab adding to his bag of sparrows, it might be a man who knew something of the neighbourhood.

There was no doubt about the direction that the sound of the shot had come from. To his left the ground fell sharply and there were two tracks branching away. The one to the right was clearly the more frequently used and within less than five minutes, Kenworthy found himself among thinning trees, looking down into a deep, steep and narrow valley. Then came another shot—very much closer now, and he was almost certain this time that it was the desiccated crack of a small-calibre automatic. Then a second one, and the whirring of a ricochet spinning off its axis. He began to whistle—*Phil the Fluter's Ball*—thinking it good policy to let the unknown hunter know that there was another human about, possibly in his line of fire.

There was a pause of some minutes before he heard another shot, and this time he saw the muzzle-smoke and the firer in the same moment. It was a woman: a neat, small-made young woman in a hooded anorak. She appeared to be firing at tree-trunks at short range. She was aiming at eye-level with her arm extended: no nonsensical cowboy stuff.

'Ahoy there! Hold your fire!'

He heard her laugh.

'All right—you're safe, Mr Kenworthy.'

It was Monique Colin, from the St Hubert, looking as fetching in her forest-walking garb as she had been in nylon fur. She joined him.

'I couldn't resist the temptation to do a little target-practice: though I only have twenty-five rounds. We don't get much opportunity to shoot—and you never know. I took this off your friend, by the way. You'd better have it. I'll leave you to judge whether to give it back to him.'

She handed him the weapon. It was a Spanish Erboa 7.65, somebody's relic of the Civil War. He remembered that Chantal Dupuy had used that phrase of the weapon that Neville had once hoped to defend the pass with.

'You took it off him? Why? Was he being murderous? Or suicidal?'

'Neither, really. Or both, possibly, I just preferred to think of him without it.'

He gave the gun back to her.

'If I'm picked up by the PJ, I don't want to be found carrying this. Where is the Colonel?'

'High up on a crevice, in a very dilapidated pile that used to be some wealthy man's taste in seclusion. He has been there before—'

'Yes. I know that story. How did you find him?'

'By asking around—in the only other place where he was likely to be. On the Montagne des Louves, at the smallholding of an elderly couple called Besson—the ones who adopted his daughter. They had hid him up for some weeks, during the war.'

'I see. And you had no difficulty, getting them to tell you?'

'I don't think they'd have told the PJ—and forgive my saying this, Monsieur Kenworthy—I doubt if they'd have told you. It takes the French to talk to the French—I do not mean linguistically, of course. This is a very French case, Monsieur Kenworthy.'

'So I've noticed. And how did you find out about the Bessons?'

'Everyone in St Blaise knew about them.'

'And does Neville know about his wife's death?'

'I broke it to him. It seemed to wash over him. He didn't seem to take it in.'

'Did he kill her, do you think?'

'I'm unsure. At some moments I think he did. At others, I think not.'

'What's he doing now?'

'Some people might say mooning about. Straightening things out in his mind: well, trying to. I doubt whether he ever will. I don't think he'll ever come to terms with himself. On short acquaintance—we didn't talk for long, but we were intense—it seems to me that all his life he's been trying to be something that he's not. Circumstances—his family, his schooling, his officer cadet course—God knows that— everything has always forced him in one direction. That's the English side of the case for you. I can't say I even begin to understand your Colonel Neville. Whew! When you bring us work in the Agence, Monsieur Kenworthy, you do face us up to the heavy artillery—first the redoubtable Fayard, then the formidable Dupuy. Do you mind if I ask you something?'

'Ask on.'

'What is your angle now, Monsieur Kenworthy?'

'Nothing, really. Except to rally round old Neville, in case I can be of use to him.'

'Yes, well—I'd do that, if I were you—on humanitarian grounds. I'd give him a little more time to himself, but it would be a kindness to get to him before nightfall. You can do it in an hour and a half from here. And as for me—do you think I might ask you a favour?'

'Anything I can possibly do—'

'Well—I can't see that you have any further concrete interest in this case. Would you leave me to try to break it?

I'm thinking of how much good it would do us in the Agence, if we could do an honest good turn for Fayard.'

'All yours,' Kenworthy said.

CHAPTER 18

'Come along, Kenworthy—you're in default. Where've you been? You don't know what you've been missing.'

Kenworthy's first interpretation was that Neville's marbles had spilled out of his reach—out of the reach of both of them. His age, the upheaval of so much unpalatable memory, the personal shock at the death of his wife: all had combined to blow the fuses of a mind that had been tempting an overload for a long time.

The Colonel had been sitting by a broken balustrade when Kenworthy first caught renewed sight of him, on the edge of a protruding jib of rock. Sixty years ago this had been an Italianate garden terrace, but any hark-back to cultivation had long since been lost. Frosts and weeds had had their way with flagstones, copings had fallen, amphorae and statuettes were crumbled and featureless. Behind were the traceable remains of a small villa, its roof open to the sky, its over-ornamentation grotesque in destruction. The valley was as desolate: the wake of the death-throes of a glacier. He climbed by a track that must surely have had the heart in the mouth of the least sensitive of muleteers.

And Neville was sitting looking out over this sterility, a man of bulk and strength, confident and humourless.

'You're panting and puffing like an old granny, Kenworthy. I'd never have believed it, but I've actually missed you.'

Kenworthy picked his way down over the fallen stones to where Neville was sitting on a broken marble bench.

'Come and make yourself comfortable. You don't know

what you've been missing. I've had a visit from a young lady who'd have made your eyeballs stand out.'

Kenworthy settled on a new interpretation of Neville's mental state. The heavy nonsense he was talking was his substitute for a sense of humour. Looking back, there was a lot of nonsense about Neville that could be explained away as the best he could do in the way of humour. What was humour, anyway? A psychological diversion for shrugging off the intolerable. Neville's mechanism must always have been defective.

And there was only one way of dealing with him. Kenworthy knew he should have used it over their first meal together in the fish-market square in Old Nice. He had to lose his temper with him, lose it so persuasively that he gained and kept the upper hand.

'Neville—I've had as much as I can take of you. And I've spent the last few days with a small group of French people who reached the same impasse forty years ago.'

Neville looked at him with solemn, hurt eyes.

'You don't know these people, Kenworthy. You can't begin to guess what the tensions were.'

'And you didn't come within a million miles of understanding the first thing about them.'

'Kenworthy—let's get a few things straight—'

As Monique Colin had said, she had not spent long with him, but her scalpel had peeled back the right membranes: Neville's incompatibility with circumstance, with his family, his schooling and his officer training. All his life he had failed—but all his life had seen himself close enough to the trappings of success to go on kidding himself. Dry-cleaning —a chain of small shops in small market-towns. Neville was probably looked up to in Rotary; with an aura of reputed past gallantry that he preferred never to discuss.

'I'd find you more convincing,' Kenworthy said, 'if I could detect the faintest tinge of grief.'

'What have I got to grieve about?'

'You were married to her for twelve years—and closely associated for most of your adult life.'

Neville laughed; or at least he made bitter noises in his throat.

'Closely associated: thank you for the phrase. And thank you for doing your homework for a change. So you know that she was my admin back-up over the years that mattered?'

'She must have been in love with you for a very long time.'

'In love? I'm not sure that I know what that means— that I ever have known. Oh yes—there are periods of excitement in our lives—mostly when we are young. I suppose Agnes went through hell the night my moondrop plane took off—and euphoria when we got a cryptic message through that I'd arrived. I was forbidden fruit while Lavinia drew breath.'

'And she waited for you.'

'She'd been married in the meanwhile: to a man who was less sentimental about integrity than I was. I don't know what she wanted from me. Power over me, I suppose. Can there be such a thing as blackmail within marital bonds? I've never heard of a case in court. I suppose it's a moot legal point. Of course, the dry-cleaning shops have always been worth something.'

'Did she know a great deal about what had happened on Le Baou—and elsewhere?'

'Did she *know*? Who ever *knew*? She surmised that she knew. And then one day a document got into her hands: the gospel according to Chantal Dupuy.'

A great bird of prey—a Bonelli's eagle, though neither man could have identified it—swooped on quarry that they could not see.

'Look, Kenworthy: I'm not saying that there weren't heroes and heroines. I'd rate Chantal Dupuy high among the claimants. She was brought to St Blaise for more than one reason. To manage my logistics, to help me with my screening job: the female touch was said to be needed. But also to assess what was happening on Le Baou, and to suggest a rationale for licking things into trim. There was a power struggle going on. Charles Levaray—a man called Combret, a Post Office Engineer, who gave us a lot of trouble—a young MO called Bézin who thought he was the only one who knew how the shoot ought to be run.'

'A *young* man called Bézin?'

'He was the one who treated my ankle. They brought him down from the backwoods somewhere. He's still about in St Blaise. I saw him in his car.'

'It sounds to me as if you're talking about Aubin.'

'Bézin. He told me his name. I heard others call him that.'

'Cover. Neville—I am not far from believing that this man Bézin—or at least the name Bézin—comes somewhere near the kernel of this affair. Every time I mentioned him to Chantal Dupuy she did her best to cover up. Aubin told me that you were attended to on Le Baou by an old doctor called Bézin. He even told me at which university he'd qualified. And in the furore following your visit, the Gestapo got on to Bézin. Bézin mixed himself a potion that saved him from something worse.'

'The Bézin who put me in plaster was a youngster, a medical student on the run, and I have seen him within the last week.'

'Accompanied by an elderly woman in nun's habit?'

'The same.'

Somewhere they heard the buzz of a chain-saw.

'We shan't solve the Bézin angle here and now,' Kenworthy said. 'Go on with your story.'

'Well, everything that could go wrong did go bloody wrong. For every reason that could crop up. Not overlooking my ineptitude. And if it's taken half a century for me to admit that to myself, I've not made this long journey for nothing.'

He looked at Kenworthy with a thin smile. Kenworthy believed that he meant what he was saying.

'But you see, I knew Pops Foster, who'd been on a walking tour with one or two of us when we were youngsters, and who had made Major-General. I pleaded with him to be sent for a lone-wolf ploy. He thought I was up to it. As you'll have worked out, I came back empty-handed. The German was murdered—'

'By—?'

'Person or persons unknown. There were plenty who were minded that way.'

'Tell me about this German.'

'Her name was Hilde Fischer-Haurath. She was a progeny of the Haurath family, the Haurath Betrieb of Ludwigshafen, industrial chemists with a solid stake in high explosives.'

'And is it true that there was an agreement between Haurath and a sister company in the UK that even straddled the worst of the war?'

'No. That is manifestly untrue. That is what Chantal thought, and we had an up-and-downer over it. She had no grounds at all for thinking that: latrine gossip. What Hilde and I were talking about was between me and my masters. In peacetime there had, it is true, been a tie-up between Haurath and a British combine, but all that was frozen in the general moratorium of September, '39. The truth of the matter was that Haurath were thinking ahead—or 'thought they were. World War Two was nothing but a preliminary knock-up. The confrontation that truly mattered was when the West took on the USSR. That was strong current thinking in a lot of German circles: witness Hess's flight to the UK. There were some who didn't think it would be long after the Nazis were knocked out. Some even thought it ought to follow straight on—while the Russians were still bled pallid. Now the Hauraths were working on something new and devastating that they were ready to bring on

stream. It was something to do with plastic explosive. Even
the working parts and outer shell of a missile could be HE.
The V2 would have been twenty times as destructive as it
was. The tentative suggestion was that if we would lay off
bombing the Haurath complex, they would make over the
formula to us. A preliminary approach was made through
Eire. And there were bods in the Ministry of Economic
Warfare who, without committing themselves, thought that
the thing ought at least to be looked at. I was sent to pick
up an abstract of the specifications from Hilde.'

'It seems an unlikely thing, to have sent a woman with
it.'

'Precisely why they did send a woman, old man. But
of course, some Frenchman with a mind of his own saw
assassination as the solution to everything. In the ensuing
free-for-all, somebody else relieved me of the formula. And
in the event, Haurath was saturation-bombed in February,
'44. You couldn't promise not to bomb the Mannheim-
Ludwigshafen complex. I. G. Farben was too close.'

'And Chantal Dupuy was pregnant.'

Neville went and leaned on one of the remaining pillars
of the balcony.

'Are you here to make moral judgements, Kenworthy?

'Not in the least. None of it's my business.'

'I spoke just now of being in love. I think this was the
only time in my life that it truly happened to me. They were
abnormal times. This was an abnormal place. And Chantal
was in love with me—whatever she may say about that
now. I can count, alas, on the fingers of my hands the
number of days and nights that we were in love. Incidentally,
I could have sworn that none of my precautions went wrong.
I'd no idea that Chantal had had a child, until I had the
letter from young Yvette.'

And Hilde Haurath? Kenworthy did not intend to pursue
that angle. But this piece of mind-reading was an obvious
one, even for a man with as many blind spots as Neville.

'I never slept with Hilde Fischer—but try telling that to Chantal Dupuy! We were up here,' Neville said. 'With one tin of pineapple to last the duration. I'd laid a false trail—it never occurred to me that I might compromise the Vittorini brothers: but that was only because the Gestapo had to bring somebody to book. All I had accomplished was to drive us into this cul-de-sac. Any patrol coming up this valley had us cold. Any ambush up in the forest had only to wait for us. I had one small pistol that was useless at more than fifteen yards—and in my hands not too reliable at that. Hilde took a lot of comforting. Then Chantal and her friends risked their lives again, scoured the valleys for us, found us here, smuggled us to the Bessons on the Montagne des Louves. Another spell of short commons!'

Neville repeated his sardonic laugh.

'I've always talked of short commons: I lived on French farm butter, unlimited cheese and eggs, roast guinea-fowl, home-cured hams, God knows what other *cochonnailles*. Eventually Le Baou picked up the message about my return journey. They took another dollop of risks and brought me back to the Rock, thence to Menton and the Royal Navy.'

'And how did Mrs Neville get to know about these goings on? Because you told her?'

'I hardly saw her at my debriefing. She was of course not allowed to sit in on it—and I had my own home to go to. That was an office you didn't go to without invitation—and I was never invited again. No: the final stroke was something I've always regarded as malice: though I didn't guess in those days that I'd left Chantal with child. During one of our major rows, she had threatened to inform London that she could no longer take responsibility for working with me. I warned her against any such course—the Establishment would never have taken her word against mine. She held her hand—but after the war, she sent a long report to London. And when I say the war was over, I don't mean May, '45. I mean autumn '44, when the Resistance had

stopped blowing trains up, and people like Chantal thought
it was all over.'

Neville took a caged animal's walk the length of the
balcony.

'She addressed her report to the War Office. Very ran-
corous it must have been, and would duly go on file and be
forgotten. I'd been smartly dropped as a parachutist, and
I've no doubt my papers were marked that I was strictly to
be put on wasting time until the Cease Fire. I suppose that
was better than sending me on a suicide errand. But Agnes
read that report. She read it and remembered it—and held
it in reserve until she needed it.'

Kenworthy lit his pipe. Neville thumped a palm with his
fist and said by God, he wished he hadn't thrown his last
pipe away.

'I've been less than fair about my marriage to Agnes,
Kenworthy. I was glad enough of it at the time, easily
persuaded myself that this was love again. And I think she
was in love with me in a retarded schoolgirl way when I
first passed through her office. When she married me, she
still thought I was more than tolerable. I don't know where
I went wrong. She wasn't the sort of woman that I could
satisfy, and I don't mean primarily in bed, though that too.
It was when she knew the mistake she had made that she
started using what she knew about me. In all fairness, I
don't think it was until after we'd been married a month or
two that she really started believing some of the things that
Chantal had written. We didn't break up. It would have
cost both of us too much. We lived separate lives within the
marriage. Mine at this time was largely concerned with
getting manufacturers to put labels in clothes saying I was
the only safe fellow to come to for cleaning. I should have
brazened it out, when she threatened to blow the gaffe to
my friends. But she could have done, you know. They knew
nothing about me, bar what I encouraged them to think.
She could have blown all that sky-high.'

'You must have been bloody careless to let her know you had heard from Yvette.'

'The letter came, forwarded from the War Office, to which the girl had written, while I was away on business. She must have steamed it open. I made up my tale about wanting to go on a walking-tour; didn't realize how smart she was going to be on the ball.'

'So what now?'

'Now? Well, I'm tired of this place for a start.' He indicated the ruin. 'I came here to recapture something. When shall I learn that it is always a mistake to try to do that? I haven't called on the Bessons yet. I don't think that's advisable either, but I think somehow I ought to complete the circuit. You see—here I go again. I'd invite you to come with me, only it's a bloody long way.'

'It's been a bloody long way all along,' Kenworthy said. 'And how about you? Are you really up to it? What about this operation of yours?'

For the third time, Neville produced his mirthless laugh.

'Operation? Hæmorrhoids. I go into a cold panic every time I think of a general anæsthetic. Hate that feeling of going off. Way I'm made, I suppose.'

They started together up the valley and presently the lower mountain slopes ahead of them were dotted with isolated farmhouses, some of them already showing twinkling spots of light.

'La Montagne des Louves, and the one at half past ten from the L-shaped rock is the Bessons' place.'

'It'll be half past ten before we get there. Who ever thought of establishing homesteads in places like that?'

Neither man had a tent. Kenworthy judged that they had between two and three hours' walking still ahead of them.

'There'll be a moon, rising about eight. We can sit it out when dusk gets too much for us. You'll be relieved to know that I have a bar of chocolate.'

They walked on until they began to stumble in the failed

light, and Neville found them a spot to rest. It was reasonably sheltered by a fold in the hillside, and there was a
stream that, though icy, was as pure as any water they were
ever likely to find. Kenworthy was stooping to lower a
cupped hand when something hard, heavy and obliterating
struck the base of his skull. Pyrotechnics: and then darkness.

CHAPTER 19

At eleven o'clock the next morning a hospital service van
drew up with two of its wheels on the narrow pavement
outside Dr Aubin's surgery. Madame Ripault was still off
duty and keeping to her room, which did not make for easy
handling of *les malades*. There were a number of cartons to
be delivered, but there was no man crouching among them.
One of the patients waiting her turn was Madame Piquemal
from Les Platanes at Fresnes les Puits, who needed something to steady her nerves.

When he had found someone to sign his waybill, the
driver made the circuit of the one-way streets down into the
Place de la Libération and found a parking space close to
the memorial to Joseph Vittorini, looking inquiringly at
the very young municipal policeman, who registered no
objection. He went into Les Tilleuls, which he found moder-
ately busy, though not until the stroke of midday would St
Blaise's garage-hands, bakers, electricians and plumbers
come crowding in for their *pastis*. At one end of the counter
an elderly man in a beret, with the ribbon of the *Légion* in
his lapel, was talking to three old men. One of them asked
him what on earth it was he was smoking.

'It's a packet that *notre petit voisin*'s friend gave me. The
first pipeful I smoked made me as dizzy as a schoolboy
behind the garden wall.'

'So it isn't all settled yet, then?'

'No. They had us all in yesterday. Oh—they were very fair, very polite, very dignified. Most of us were back home before nightfall. *Le docteur* was the last they brought back—but that was only because he made the longest statement.'

'And Mademoiselle Dupuy?'

'Gone back to Nantes already. She has a case opening tomorrow.'

Outside, there was an absence of certain faces that had made themselves memorable yesterday. Inspector Fayard had called off the plainclothes men whom he had had dotted about here and in Fresnes. Or, that is to say, if Fayard had men here, they were men with different faces and in different guises. A true connoisseur of French sleuths might have regarded as highly suspect two individuals at one of the café terrace tables who scanned every car that passed to make sure they could account for who was in it.

Kenworthy woke up in hospital, not for the first time—he had been waking at bewildering intervals all night, and feared that he might have been talking all kinds of rubbish. Each time he came to, he had had to pick his way through a painful kaleidoscope: every movement of his eyes seemed to send skewer-hot jabs through the back of his skull. At one moment he was in a French farmhouse kitchen, smelling of home-cured tobacco and vegetable broth and Gauloise cigarettes. And the farmer was so old and white-moustached that Kenworthy took him to be a former *poilu* of the First World War. Then he was in an ambulance, and he thought that Dr Boillot had put him in it to get him away from Fresnes. And then Dr Boillot himself was there, and he resented Dr Boillot; because it somehow impinged on his consciousness that Boillot had sent the young woman away. What was she doing here, anyway? There were odd happy moments when her face, looking down at him, close to him, seemed to fill his existence. Only her perfume was too much for him. It made him feel sick—and that had certainly not been the case the first time he had smelled it. In Nice. In a workaday *quartier* south-east of the station.

He must be feeling more reasonable this morning, or the middle of this afternoon, or whatever, because it did occur to him that one of the courses open to him was to call a nurse and ask what the hell had happened to him.

'I wouldn't try lifting your head off the pillow, if I were you, Monsieur Kenworthy.'

A voice from a bedside chair: *her* voice. He turned, and she smiled at him, which began to melt him inside—until he realized that even trying to move his neck was not to be advised.

The woman from the Agence St Hubert—he had trouble at first remembering her name—Monique—Monique Colin —got up from the chair.

'I'll go and get Dr Boillot.'

Who would immediately send her away again, as he had done before, as he kept on doing.

'No,' Kenworthy said. 'No—'

But he abandoned his protest. It involved too much talking. He surrendered to the hospital routine of letting things happen. A nurse came and gave him some jalop or other. Then Monique Colin came, with Boillot, then she went away of her own accord, and Boillot came to the bedside and tortured him, like peering into the backs of his eyes with a strong light.

'You'll be relieved to know, Monsieur Kenworthy, that nothing is broken—not even a hair-crack. You must have a skull like armour-plating. Mind you, it did help that your friend's handy with a pistol—she tells me she'd actually got in some target-practice in the woods yesterday morning.'

Kenworthy remembered that. And he remembered that bloody imbecile Neville, whom he'd allowed to persuade him to start a marathon walk in gathering twilight up a primeval valley without a footpath.

'I'm afraid you're going to have a sore head for a day or

two. And you're not going to enjoy cerebration. So don't
cerebrate. No one will come near you till I say so.'

'Only Mademoiselle Colin. I'd better say thank-you to
Mademoiselle Colin.'

'OK. I'll send her along. But thank-you is only two
syllables in French. You're restricted to *merci* for the time
being. You've got enough to contend with, without that sort
of excitement.'

Fayard's team had reconstructed Agnes Neville's act, which
needed patience and a great deal of telephoning. Her name
was in an Air France passenger manifest. It was on a
registration slip in a hotel from which she certainly could
not have observed the deployment of a fish-stall. Finding
the taxi that had driven her up la Montagne was more
laborious, but bore fruit eventually. So eventually Fayard
knew how she had reached the Bessons', which had involved
a quarter of a mile on foot down a track for which her
footwear could not be regarded as sensible. All of this had
to be established, but it proved to be of no more material
use than Fayard had expected it to be. Agnes Neville had
arrived in Nice, she had overnighted in Nice, she had had
herself driven to where she wanted to go. She had been
killed there, by a stone thrown from close quarters at the
back of her skull, and the time of death was deduced as
early evening.

Fayard had also checked and cross-checked the movements of those who had made expeditions out of St Blaise
on the afternoon in question. Aubin and Chantal Dupuy
had called together on the Bessons, expecting Neville to be
there, but finding that this was not the case, they had stayed
less than an hour. Levaray had been dropped along the road
outside St Blaise and had climbed the hillside up towards
Le Baou. Madame Ripault had gone on alone in that car,
and had arrived at Les Carreaux as Dupuy and the doctor
were leaving. She stayed half an hour. During that half-hour

the garage-hand, who had driven her, and his inseparable Yvette, wandered out of sight along a field footpath, and did not appear to have seen very much except each other. Progress nil.

Fayard caused consternation by putting up at Les Platanes, waiting in his room for the phone to bring him word from the detective who was on the spot at the hospital. No word came.

As soon as she was back from Aubin's surgery, Madame Piquemal went shopping in Fresnes les Puits, bought a basket of fruit sufficient to feed a family for a week, and carried it personally along the Tanguy road to Kenworthy. She was highly indignant that she was not allowed to see him.

Kenworthy came out of his current dose of sedation fairly late in the evening and badly needed a cool drink. Monique Colin, who was quietly reading by his bed, gave him one. This time he put together more easily his reasons for being here, though there were still frightening gaps. He wanted to talk, and Monique Colin discouraged him. She also made a discreet signal to the nursing staff that he was ready for a new round of their cruel attentions.

As is common in cases of concussion, he had no memory of an actual incident, or of the minutes leading up to it. Walking up the valley, seething with fury at his stupidity in letting Neville get him in tow again—

'Was it Neville who clobbered me?'

'No, not Neville. Someone threw a boulder at your head,' Monique said. 'While you were trying to get a drink from the stream: someone who came out of the shadows. It was someone I'd followed down, after I'd been to see the Bessons. Because I guessed you'd be coming up there sooner or later. And I didn't see who it was—I heard, rather than saw. Then I fired, winged whoever it was, threw her off her aim. So all you got really was a glancing blow.'

'That's all I got, is it? Thank God for that mercy.'

'Rest, now, Monsieur Kenworthy. And perhaps to-morrow—'

Kenworthy did try to rest, but opened his eyes again on a recurrent thought.

'Mademoiselle—there is an anomaly.'

'Yes—there are several.'

'No. This is special. I break all my best cases on anomalies.'

He had to struggle to remember a French name.

'Don't torment yourself, Monsieur Kenworthy.'

Then it came.

'Bézin. Why did Dr Aubin tell Colonel Neville, when he came to treat his ankle on Le Baou, that his name was Bézin?'

'I'm sure it does not matter.'

'And I'm sure it does.'

He made two or three false starts before he got out the story coherently. Boillot had come into the ward while he was in the middle of it and came over at something he heard.

'What's all this about Bézin?'

Kenworthy told him, Monique helping. Boillot's face was grimmer than Kenworthy had ever seen it.

'This puts a different complexion on everything,' he said.

A night's repose—give or take a few hallucinations. But there must have been deep rest, too, because in the morning he felt many shades better. Boillot did not come to see him. The houseman who attended to him was conservative, and would not depart from Boillot's orders in the most trivial detail. Monique did not come to see him until very late.

'It occurs to me,' he said, 'that Boillot has played more than a walking-on part in all this. Who is he, and where does he fit in?'

'A friend of the family. That's how he puts it.'

'Yes—that's what he said to me.'

'They've always been close, the medical fraternity round here: Bézin, Aubin, Madame Ripault, Boillot—it's almost a freemasonry.'

It sounded as if Monique had been busier than she was very ready to admit.

'Boillot was not in the Resistance with the rest of them. He's rather a younger man—with a great admiration for what went on in those days. At least he says he *had* an admiration—'

'Do I scent a pending dénouement?'

'Now don't you trouble your head about anything.'

'Are you going out of your way to be frustrating?'

'Suffice it to say that Fayard found your anomaly fascinating. He asked me to thank you.'

She left him, had not come back by mid-afternoon. Just before four o'clock a nurse approached with the look that nurses wear when heralding surprise, surprise. He heard female soles and heels coming down the ward. Elspeth.

'Now what have you been getting up to?'

The world she brought with her seemed almost unreal. The real world was St Blaise, Fresnes les Puits, Le Baou. In the middle of what had to be said—and in the gaps when neither could find much to say—he saw, over his wife's shoulder, Monique come in. Monique caught sight of Elspeth, turned to go. Kenworthy beckoned her with a motion of his head that caused him to see blue lights and silver stars.

'Darling—may I introduce my sister-in-arms?'

'You're speaking metaphorically, I hope?'

It was evident within seconds that Elspeth liked Monique: though she was to make sly cracks about her for some months to come.

'The trouble is,' Monique said, 'there's no short way of telling it.'

'You'll have to tell it the long way, then,' Elspeth said. 'He'll never get better till he knows it all.'

'There's so much in their history that they can't afford to have known to their world. In Chantal Dupuy's because she killed Hilde Haurath. Oh, she was no stranger to death. One German less, what did that matter? Thanks to her and her bravery there were several hundred Germans less. She was convinced at the time that she was morally right. Democracy was cleaner without the sort of contract that she truly believed Hilde Fischer and Neville were here to draw up. Then she had stolen the abstract that had meant so much to Neville. She has it still, among her papers in Brittany. And Aubin was responsible for the death of Bézin. Even Boillot did not know that until you came out with your famous anomaly.'

Kenworthy's head was beginning to swim. It got worse as he fought not to show it.

'Levaray had brought Aubin down from the mountain to attend to Neville, and he told Neville his name was Bézin, because as Aubin he was a hunted man. It was also partly a weak in-joke, because Bézin—a greatly loved man—was getting on in years. Most of those who heard him say it understood that. But there were men on Le Baou who knew nothing about St Blaise personalities. They thought he *was* Bézin. Someone who was picked up later leaked to the Gestapo. Bézin was arrested. And Aubin let that happen— pure cowardice, made worse by the fact that he pleaded self-justification. Bézin was old; himself, he had a lifetime of service to mankind ahead of him.'

'Just a moment: someone must have had an urge to confess. Chantal?'

'No—she's back in Nantes. There are some who would say that that shows character. The temptation to stay within observing distance of Fayard must have been very great. No: this is from Madame Ripault.'

'I have never really known who she is.'

'She was a lay sister in a nursing order. During the war, she did wonderful undercover work in the mountains, but she was ultimately asked to leave the convent. And that was because of a crush she had on a young houseman: Marcel Aubin. Madame Ripault never came to proper terms with her difficulties. She never forgave herself for not being allowed to take her full vows. Nevertheless she could not bring herself to renounce Aubin. He simply did not love her. There has never been anything between them—except for her management of his professional life.'

'Albeit often a pain in the neck,' Kenworthy said.

'All useful people are a pain in the neck from time to time. The *juge d'instruction* had given Fayard plenary powers, what we call *une commission rogatoire,* since he clearly could not himself tackle all the on-the-spot investigations. In spite of this, Fayard thought he'd better arm himself with a mandate to search before paying his visit to the surgery this morning. Aubin had been difficult enough on the previous occasion, when it had been purely and simply a matter of establishing that she really was suffering from nervous prostration. This time Fayard believed that he was going to discover something more. But while he was away in Nice, getting his warrant, I rang the surgery bell as a make-believe patient. The house was so disorganized, with La Ripault off duty, that I had no difficulty in finding her bedroom. I found her in bed, with a dressing on a wounded left shoulder. A nasty little 7.65 had had to be dug out of the muscle.'

'Fayard must have been furious to find you there.'

'Why should he be? I handed him La Ripault on a plate. He might have hesitated to tear off a woman's bandage, but there's nothing squeamish about me.'

'And you mean it was Madame Ripault who hurled that boulder at my head? I thought she was in Nice, under *instruction.*'

'She was one of the first that the magistrate dismissed. And she hired a car out to the Bessons again.'

'With the express purpose of throwing a boulder at me?'

'Don't take it personally,' Monique Colin said.

'Attempted murder never is a personal matter, of course.'

'She attacked you first, I suppose, because you were bending to the water. She would undoubtedly have gone for Neville immediately. She was determined to liquidate anyone whose presence would have brought out the squalid little truths of those war years. Very jealous of the good name of her medical practice in La Ripault. A medical student who sheltered behind another doctor's name, a pregnant public prosecutor who murdered an entrusted contact—to say nothing of a career officer who's still afraid that a post-war commission of inquiry might cashier him retrospectively—'

The Kenworthys sat in the departure lounge of Nice airport, watching an occasional chopper of the Monte Carlo shuttle.

'It seems to me,' Elspeth said, 'that nobody has told me yet why Agnes Neville came to France.'

'To kill her husband—if she had to. Or anybody else, if there was no other way of influencing them.'

'Just so that she and her daughter wouldn't be done out of their inheritance?'

'They could have lost significantly. Neville did well out of dry cleaning.'

'Wouldn't it have been simpler to have stayed at home and killed him?

'Hardly. She'd have been the only suspect. That poor idiot Neville hadn't an enemy in the world.'

Later they watched the main building of the Côte d'Azur Aéroport recede to the skyline. A dozen rows in front of them the head and neck of an elderly British Colonel held themselves bull-like and erect. It was the second time that Neville had settled in his seat. The first time, he had misread his seat reservation and an air hostess had had to move him to the other side of the plane to avoid splitting up a family.

THE END